1—Paddletail the Beaver

PADDLETAIL THE BEAVER AND
HIS NEIGHBORS

Paddletail, Mrs. Paddletail, Brownie, and Silver lived
in the Black Forest on the Old Homestead.

OLD HOMESTEAD
TALES
VOLUME 3

Paddletail the

BEAVER

and His Neighbors

by NEIL WAYNE NORTHEY

Drawings by William Wilke

ORGINALLY PUBLISHED BY:
PACIFIC PRESS PUBLISHING
BOISE, ID
RE-PUBLISHED BY:
A.B. PUBLISHING
ITHACA, MI
COVER ART AND DESIGN BY:
JAMES CONVERSE
COPYRIGHT 1998

Old Homestead Tales Series

Contents

Introduction

IF you have read the books *The Bluebirds and Their Neighbors* and *The Mallards and Their Neighbors* you have already heard about many of the Feathered Friends and Furry Friends on the Old Homestead.

In the first book we told you about the birds and animals that lived near the Grand Old House and in the Apple Orchard and the Green Meadow and the Hedgerow. They were the ones that were not so timid as others, but liked to stay near human habitation.

In the second book we told you about the Furry Friends and Feathered Friends that lived at the Duck Pond and along Little River. They were the ones that liked to stay near water.

In both of these books we mentioned the Black Forest on the Old Homestead, and no doubt you have wanted to hear more about the little Wild Creatures who lived there. So in this book you will read about the more Timid Friends, who liked to live in the seclusion of the Black Forest near Paddletail the Beaver's Wildwood Pond where Fearful the Man seldom came.

Sometimes I think how good it will be in the New Earth, when God's Creatures will no longer try to hide from Fearful the Man, but will trust him and trust one another as they did in the Garden of Eden.

We may think that the little Wild Creatures are not kind to one another, when we read about how they steal from and even kill one another; but, after all, Fearful the Man is the worst enemy they have; so they sneak away and hide whenever he comes near.

If we always remember that God loves His little Wild Creatures so much that He knows when even a sparrow falls, I am sure that we will be kind to them, for we will not want Him to see us do anything to them that His Son Jesus would not have done while He was here on earth.

Of course some of the little Wild Creatures are criminals, and we should help to protect others from them even though we would rather let them live. But before we convict any criminal we should first know something about him. If we study the little Wild Creatures we shall find all kinds of characteristics among them. Some are musicians; others are weather forecasters; some are civil engineers; and we find even masons, weavers, miners, hunters, swimmers, and, of course, aviators among them.

So, before we can tell which ones are criminals and which are not, we must become acquainted with them as any wise judge would do. We hope that after reading about the little Wild Creatures in our stories you will want to meet all these Feathered Friends and Furry Friends yourself.

THE AUTHOR.

Denver, Colorado.

CHAPTER 1

Paddletail's Home in the Black Forest

"OH, dear, I do wish that tree would fall down!" said Paddletail the Beaver to Mrs. Paddletail. Then he buried his long teeth in the Troublesome Tree and gave his body a strong lunge, but still the Troublesome Tree refused to come down.

Paddletail the Beaver had chewed off a large tree with which to repair his High Dam, as he had done many times; but instead of falling kersplash into the water, it had tumbled against another tree; and there it was.

Paddletail looked the situation over as any good workman would have done. "Well, I'll have to cut that other tree so they will both fall down," he said. And down under the water dived Paddletail the Beaver to start his cutting.

Perhaps you will think it was queer that trees should be growing out of water, and you may also wonder why Paddletail's first tree did not fall, seeing that he was such an expert workman. You may be sure that there was a good reason for both.

When Paddletail and Mrs. Paddletail had come

to the Black Forest to make their home, they had decided to build a High Dam across Little River, and that would make a Wildwood Pond in which they could swim and float logs. So they had set to work and had built a High Dam across Little River, and soon their High Dam was making a Wildwood Pond.

Now it happened that there were many, many trees growing along Little River, as they grew along the same Little River where it flowed through the Old Homestead not far away, and, of course, when the Wildwood Pond filled with water it flooded the ground where the trees were standing. That was why Paddletail the Beaver had to dive under the water whenever he wanted to cut one of the trees, and that was why Paddletail's tree had fallen against the other. Who could tell where his tree was falling if he was working under water as Paddletail was? But Paddletail the Beaver made a few mistakes, and after he had cut off the other tree, down came both of them kersplash! Then he went about his business of repairing his High Dam.

"That was a fine job of tree cutting," said someone near by. Paddletail looked up, and there sat Peter Cottontail.

"Not a good one, I should say," replied Paddle-

"I do wish that tree would fall down!" said Paddletail.

tail. "You see, while I was working under the water I became turned around a bit, and I felled that first tree right into another. Or it may have been that the Playful Air Whiffs came along then and blew it the wrong way."

"I suppose you are repairing your High Dam," said Peter; "though it looks all right to me."

"Yes, I am fixing my High Dam," said Paddletail. "It is not quite high enough to suit me; and, besides, I fear it is not strong enough to hold if the Warm Spring Rains make many Singing Rivulets and all of them try to flow down Little River together. No, sir; I am afraid the High Dam would not hold."

"It would be too bad if a Foaming Flood came and washed it all away," said Peter.

"Oh, it would not wash away all of the High

(13)

Dam," said Paddletail. "You see, I leave a weak place in it, and if a Foaming Flood comes along, the weak place gives way and lets the water through. Then, after the Foaming Flood has passed, I can repair the break easily."

"That is a good idea," said Peter.

Paddletail bit off a piece of Soft Poplar Wood and sat up in the water to eat the bark from it. To Peter that looked like a strange thing to eat. But, then, Peter ate some queer things sometimes himself. He even chewed the bark from Farmer Smith's fruit trees if other food was scarce. Even though Paddletail ate bark and Tender Buds, he had his own ideas regarding what kind of trees he liked. He liked Soft Poplar Trees and Bitter Willow Trees and Cottonwood Trees and Quaking Aspen Trees and other soft trees. But Paddletail never ate the Tall Spruce Trees or the Great Pine Trees or any of the other kinds of Evergreen Trees that grew along Little River. No, sir; he did not like pitchy trees.

Sometimes when Paddletail was eating or cutting down trees, he got slivers between his teeth. Then how do you suppose he removed them? Why, with his pincers, of course. On each of Paddletail's hind feet was one toenail that was split, and it made the handiest kind of tweezers for pulling out slivers. Sometimes Paddletail used it for a comb for his hair.

"How is everyone on the Old Homestead?" asked Paddletail, for it had been a long time since he had seen Peter.

Peter never went to the Black Forest during winter because he feared that Shaggy the Wolf or Shadow the Lynx might catch him. He preferred to stay near his Friendly Burrow in the Little Jungle Thicket near the foot of High Cliff, and eat alfalfa that Bud and Mary Smith left for him and Molly.

Peter bit off a Tender Grass Shoot and sat up while he ate it. "I think everyone on the Old Homestead is all right," he said. "Molly went down to the Green Meadow to hunt for Tender Green Things, and I came over here to the Big Jungle Thicket in the Black Forest. Of course I'll be going back one of these days, when the Tender Grass Shoots begin to grow in our own Little Jungle Thicket."

"I suppose that will not be long now," said Paddletail, "for already the Pussy Willows are putting out Silky Little Buds."

"Yes, and yesterday I saw Mr. Bluebird, which means that Jolly Spring must be near. But I did not get to talk with Mr. Bluebird, for Sharpshin the Hawk almost caught him, and would have if Scrapper the Kingbird had not interfered."

"I suppose the Bluebirds will live on the Old Homestead again this year," said Paddletail.

"Oh, yes," said Peter. "Bud Smith has made them a new Nesting Box and put it on an iron post near the Grand Old House so Hunting Cat cannot climb to it. But it would be like Noisy the English Sparrow to claim it."

"Yes, I suppose so," said Paddletail; "but I must go to work, for there come Mrs. Paddletail and the Little Paddletails."

CHAPTER 2

Paddletail Enlarges His Dam

IT would be hard to say how long Paddletail the Beaver and Peter Cottontail would have visited if Mrs. Paddletail had not appeared. There was Paddletail eating Soft Poplar Bark and listening to Peter, while Peter nibbled Tender Grass Shoots and told him about the Old Homestead.

You see, although the Black Forest where Paddletail lived was really a part of the Old Homestead, yet Paddletail never went near the Grand Old House or the Rambling Old Barn or the Apple Orchard. Once the Paddletails had visited the Duck Pond, but they preferred to live in the Black Forest where there were more trees from which they could eat the bark, and where they felt more secluded.

The Paddletails were rather timid, because they feared Trapper Jim. They did not know that Friendly Folk had made laws to stop Trapper Jim from catching Beavers, and they did not know that Farmer Smith would not permit any trapping on the Old Homestead if he knew it, except for Ranger the Coyote and Snoop the Weasel and Reddy

Fox and Shaggy the Wolf and other Furry Folk that caught his chickens. But the Paddletails felt quite safe in the Black Forest.

When Paddletail saw Mrs. Paddletail coming, he decided it was time to go to work. There he was supposed to be repairing the High Dam, and all he had done was to cut down two trees. So Paddletail started immediately to trim those trees as neatly as Bud Smith could have done it with an ax.

"My, but you are getting slow!" said Mrs. Paddletail, and she cut off a limb herself. Brownie Paddletail and his sister Silver were not large enough to do much work, but how they could eat Soft Poplar Bark!

When Paddletail had finished trimming the trees, he carried the limbs to the High Dam one at a time and stuck them into the brushy top. Then he brought much moss and packed it into the brush. After that he had to bring clay, and plaster his dam so the water would not run through it.

Paddletail knew where there was some clay that was the kind he needed. It was soft and slick and waterproof. It was across the Wildwood Pond near the place where Little River flowed into the pond, and away went Paddletail swimming as fast as he could. Paddletail's hind feet had webs between the toes almost like Mr. Mallard's, and he could speed through the water swiftly. Soon he was returning with a large ball of clay, which he held against his chest under his chin with his front feet.

Brownie and Silver Paddletail were having a fine time while Paddletail was repairing the High Dam. Of course Paddletail could not get all his work done in one night or in two. He had to cut more trees and pull more moss from the bottom of the Wildwood Pond, and he carried many loads of clay with which to plaster it.

Each evening, as the Long Shadows were creeping through the Black Forest, Paddletail would start to work. Soon Mrs. Paddletail and Brownie and Silver Paddletail would arrive at the dam also, and after the Young Paddletails had

Soon he was returning
with a large ball of clay.

eaten their breakfast of Soft Poplar Bark and Tender Buds they would play Dive. Evening was a queer time to be eating breakfast, but they had been sleeping all day, so it really was their breakfast.

Mrs. Paddletail helped to repair the High Dam also, for the Beavers were a busy family. They worked most of the time; that is, when they were not playing Dive. They were repairing their High Dam, or they were cutting down trees for food, or they were fixing their Hidden Den, or they were digging Secluded Ditches.

"I believe I will make some more Secluded Ditches," said Paddletail one day, after he had finished fixing his High Dam.

"That is a good idea," said Mrs. Paddletail, "for we are badly in need of some."

You see, Paddletail had many Secluded Ditches along the edge of his Wildwood Pond. The Secluded Ditches ran back into the Jungle Thickets that grew near by. Then when he wanted some of the trees that grew there, Paddletail cut them down in such a way that they fell toward one of his Secluded Ditches, after which he cut them up into logs and floated them down the Secluded Ditch to his Wildwood Pond. If Shaggy the Wolf or some other enemy came along while Paddletail was at work, all Paddletail had to do was to dive into a Secluded Ditch and escape.

When Paddletail repaired his High Dam, and the water in his Wildwood Pond grew higher and higher, all his old Secluded Ditches were covered with water. That was why Paddletail wanted to dig more. So he set to work to make a Secluded Ditch to a certain grove of Bitter Willow Trees that grew near by.

"Aha," said Shaggy the Wolf, when he saw Paddletail starting to make a Secluded Ditch, "I'll wait and catch him before he gets it finished."

Shaggy the Wolf thought that Paddletail would be so busy digging he would forget to watch for enemies, and that would be a good time to catch him. Besides, Paddletail would not have a Secluded Ditch into which he could jump and escape until he had it finished. Shaggy the Wolf could not catch Paddletail or the Young Paddletails while they were in the water, because they could swim too swiftly. But the Paddletails could not run fast on land. They could not run nearly so fast as Shaggy, and he knew it. He knew that if he could find them cutting a tree or building a Secluded Ditch or exploring a Big Tree Grove away from water, he would have no trouble to catch them.

CHAPTER 3

Danny Muskrat Is in Trouble

DANNY MUSKRAT was worried. It was not because he was afraid enemies might catch him, or that he could not find enough to eat, or that someone might try to take his home away from him. Oh, no; it was not any of those things that worried Danny Muskrat. The thing that worried him was that his Hidden Den was filling with water.

You see, Danny Muskrat had made his Hidden Den in the Clay Bank of Paddletail's Wildwood Pond in the Black Forest. Danny had liked the Wildwood Pond the first time he had seen it, so he had made a Hidden Den in the Clay Bank. It had Secret Tunnels in it and a Secret Doorway that led to it under water. No one would ever have guessed where Danny's Hidden Den was.

Then one day Mrs. Muskrat came home excited. "Oh, dear," she said, "Paddletail the Beaver is building his High Dam higher, and I know it will flood us out."

Sure enough, when Paddletail's High Dam grew higher, the water in the Wildwood Pond grew higher, and soon Danny Muskrat's Hidden Den was filling.

"Oh, dear; oh, dear!" said Mrs. Muskrat. "What shall we do?"

Of course Paddletail the Beaver did not know that he was causing the Muskrats all that trouble. He thought he was making a better Wildwood Pond, and so he was. But even if he had known it, it really was *his* Wildwood Pond, and he had a right to make it larger if he wished to do so.

But there was Paddletail making his High Dam higher, and all the time Danny Muskrat's Hidden Den was filling with water.

"I wonder how high Paddletail will build his High Dam," said Mrs. Muskrat.

"I wonder," said Danny. But Danny and Mrs. Muskrat did not have to wonder long, for soon their Hidden Den was so full of water that they could no longer live in it.

"Now where do you suppose we can sleep to-day?" asked Mrs. Muskrat. The Laughing Yellow Sun was coming up over back of the Old Homestead, and that meant that it was time for the Muskrats and other Furry Folk who sleep during the day to go to bed.

Danny Muskrat sat on a Floating Log and looked thoughtful. "I am sure I do not know where we can sleep," he said; "but we'll be able to find some place."

"Let's swim over to Paddletail's High Dam and perhaps we can find a place in it where we can hide today," suggested Mrs. Muskrat.

"I suppose we may as well do that," said Danny, and away they swam toward Paddletail's High Dam.

Suddenly Mrs. Muskrat spied a Large Brush Pile. It was near the Clay Bank of the Wildwood Pond, and Mrs. Muskrat could see one end of a Warm Hollow Log sticking out from the midst of the brush.

"Oh, let's stay in that Warm Hollow Log today," she said.

Danny Muskrat sat on a floating log and looked thoughtful.

"Sniff, sniff,"
went Danny, as he
stopped at the Warm Hollow Log.

"That would be a good place," said Danny, "a very good place."

Up the Clay Bank scrambled Danny followed closely by Mrs. Muskrat. The Muskrats swam so much that they could not walk fast. Danny stopped at the Warm Hollow Log and sniffed. The Playful Air Whiffs told him that someone was already in there. "Sniff, sniff," went Danny; "that smells like Peter Cottontail to me."

Mrs. Muskrat waddled to the end of the Warm Hollow Log and sniffed also. "Yes, sir; that surely is Peter. Now what do you suppose he is doing over here in the Black Forest?" The Muskrats had met Peter before when he had been visiting in the

Black Forest, and that was how they knew it was Peter.

"I wonder if he would care if we slept in the Warm Hollow Log today," said Danny.

It happened that Peter had crawled into the Warm Hollow Log to sleep also, and when he heard the Muskrats sniffing at the end of it, his heart almost stopped. Peter thought that surely Trailer the Mink had found him and that he would not be able to escape. You see, the Warm Hollow Log had only one doorway, and Peter knew that he could never get out if Trailer was standing in it. You may be sure that Peter felt much better when he found out that it was only Danny and Mrs. Muskrat.

"Come right in," said Peter, for he knew that if the Muskrats were in the Warm Hollow Log with him, Trailer the Mink would never dare to come in. "What are you doing away from your Hidden Den?"

"Paddletail the Beaver has made his High Dam higher, and has flooded us out," said Mrs. Muskrat; "and now we do not know what to do."

"And what are you doing here?" asked Danny.

Peter wiggled his nose and moved farther back into the Warm Hollow Log so the Muskrats could get in. "I came over to the Black Forest because

the Tender Grass Shoots peep out of the ground
here first," said Peter; "but I like it better in our
own Little Jungle Thicket near the Grand Old
House after the Tender Green Things begin to
grow."

"Tell us about your Little Jungle Thicket and
the Old Homestead," said Mrs. Muskrat.

"Yes, do," urged Danny.

"Well, you see, Molly and I live in a Friendly
Burrow in Little Jungle Thicket," began Peter.
"Our Little Jungle Thicket is near the foot of
High Cliff where Aquila the Golden Eagle lives.
It is not a great way from the Grand Old House
where Bud and Mary Smith live. Then there is
the Rambling Old Barn where Farmer Smith
keeps Old Sorrel, and just across the Green Mea-

Aquila the Golden Eagle
lived on High Cliff.

dow is the Wide-Wide Pasture where Old Bent Horn lives. Then, near the Green Meadow is the Duck Pond where another Danny Muskrat lives; and near the Wide-Wide Pasture is the Woodlot where Virginia Opossum has her home in a Warm Hollow Log. Little River winds through the Green Meadow and the Wide-Wide Pasture, and near the Bridge that crosses it is Billy Coon's Hollow Den Tree. My nearest neighbor is Johnny Chuck, who has a Friendly Burrow on the side of High Cliff. Yes, I like the Old Homestead," said Peter, and he stretched out in the Warm Hollow Log as if he were ready to go to sleep.

CHAPTER 4

Danny Muskrat Hunts a New Location

O F course when Peter Cottontail went to sleep, there was nothing for Danny Muskrat and Mrs. Muskrat to do but to try to sleep also.

"I don't like to sleep in this Warm Hollow Log one bit," complained Mrs. Muskrat. "It's too light in here with the sun shining outside."

"Neither do I," agreed Danny; "but I don't know of a better place."

You see, the Muskrats were used to sleeping in their Hidden Den where no light could come in. No doubt Peter thought it was a fine place. Sometimes he slept in a Cozy Form under a Rabbit Bush, and he did not mind the light at all. You may be sure that the Muskrats were glad when the Laughing Yellow Sun bowed out of sight in the Golden West and once again they could go to the Wildwood Pond.

Down to the Wildwood Pond waddled Danny and Mrs. Muskrat, while Peter hopped around in front of the Warm Hollow Log and nibbled the Tender Grass Shoots that he found. As soon as it was dark enough, away went Peter toward the Big

Jungle Thicket, thumpety, thumpety, thump, as fast as he could run.

The Muskrats swam along the bank of the Wildwood Pond, looking for a breakfast of Juicy Water Bulbs. Of course, the high water had covered them deeply, but it was no trouble at all for the Muskrats to dive down to them. Then after they had found a Juicy Water Bulb, they would sit on a Floating Log, or they would climb out of the water in a Secluded Little Nook, and eat it. And all the time they were wondering where they could find a place to live.

"Let's swim around the Wildwood Pond and see if we can find a place for a new home," said Mrs. Muskrat.

"That is a good idea, a very good idea," said Danny, and away they swam along the edge of the Wildwood Pond, kicking up as they went, Silvery Ripples where the Smiling Moon touched them.

On one side of the Wildwood Pond was a Marshy Bank where Fuzzy Cattails and Swamp Grass grew. Some of them were covered with water since Paddletail had repaired his High Dam, but many of them had been growing higher on the Marshy Bank, and they were not covered.

Mrs. Muskrat swam around among the Fuzzy Cattails. She liked the Marshy Bank very much.

Trailer hid in a
clump of Tumbled Bul-
rushes and watched.

"Oh, let us build a Grassy House!" she exclaimed. "This is such a fine place, and there are
plenty of Fuzzy Cattails and Swamp Grass and
Green Moss with which to build it."

"All right," said Danny, and soon the Muskrats
were busy building a new Grassy House.

First they made a large flat pile of Swamp Grass
and Fuzzy Cattails and Green Moss right in the
water. It was so high that it was above the water
almost a foot. You see, Danny liked his house to
be entirely surrounded by water, because then
Furry Enemies could not get to it so easily. So
he built it quite a way from the Marshy Bank.

"Now, I think that will make a good floor."
said Danny, when the large, flat pile of Swamp

Grass and Fuzzy Cattails and Green Moss was high enough above the water to suit him.

Right in the center of Danny's floor was a hole, and what do you suppose he had left it there for? Why, it was Danny's door, of course. And in the Oozy Mud under the large, flat pile was a Secret Tunnel that led to the doorway. Then when Danny Muskrat wanted to get into his Grassy House, he could dive to the Secret Tunnel, follow it to the doorway, and come up right in the center of his floor.

When Danny and Mrs. Muskrat had finished their floor, they started to make a Grassy House on it. They carried more Swamp Grass and Fuzzy Cattails and Green Moss, and made walls around the edge of their floor. Their house was to be round, like a large, round basket turned upside down; but it was much larger than a basket.

Danny really had two rooms in his Grassy House. In one of them he built a Snug Bed of Swamp Grass and Green Moss. The other was his dining room, where he could sit during cold weather while he ate Sweet Cattail Stalks and Juicy Water Bulbs. You see, when Old Man Winter froze the Wildwood Pond, Danny had to hunt for food under the ice. He could not crawl out of the water onto a Floating Log or into a Secluded

Little Nook to eat it. So he carried it to his dining room in his Grassy House. Sometimes Danny kept a supply of Sweet Cattail Stalks and Juicy Water Bulbs in his dining room, so he would have something to eat if he could not find much under the ice.

One night while the Muskrats were working on their Grassy House, along came Trailer the Mink on the Marshy Bank.

"Aha," he said to himself; "I see the Muskrats are building a new Grassy House. I believe I will wait until Danny goes away after a load of Fuzzy Cattails or Swamp Grass, and then I will surprise Mrs. Muskrat."

So Trailer the Mink hid in a clump of Tumbled Bulrushes and watched. He was afraid to bother the Muskrats while both of them were at home, but he thought that after Danny left he would swim out and pounce on Mrs. Muskrat. Trailer knew that the Muskrats had long, sharp teeth, and that they would fight fiercely if they had to. Danny Muskrat seldom picked a quarrel with anyone. He would rather live in peace if he was not bothered. But Danny did not hesitate to use his strong teeth to defend himself if he had to. Trailer the Mink knew that two against one would be too many. So he waited for Danny to leave.

CHAPTER 5

Trailer the Mink Interferes

"I BELIEVE I will swim over to the edge of the Fuzzy Cattail Patch and get a load for our Grassy House," said Danny Muskrat.

"That's a good idea," said Mrs. Muskrat, "for we do not want to cut all of them down around our home."

Away swam Danny after a load of material with which to build his Grassy House. Of course Trailer the Mink was watching, and as soon as Danny was out of sight, into the water slipped Trailer as quietly as possible, and started to swim toward Mrs. Muskrat.

Mrs. Muskrat was busy piling up the Fuzzy Cattails and Swamp Grass and Green Moss that Danny had brought. She was making the walls of her bedroom, so she would have a place to sleep when the Laughing Yellow Sun came up the next morning. She was so busy that she did not see Trailer the Mink until he was almost to her Grassy House. Then she noticed that someone was making Silvery Ripples in the water, and the Silvery Ripples were coming nearer.

"Is that you, Danny?" asked Mrs. Muskrat, for she thought perhaps Danny had changed his mind about going to the other side of the Fuzzy Cattail Patch.

Trailer the Mink did not answer. He wanted to get as close as possible before Mrs. Muskrat knew it was he. Soon Mrs. Muskrat saw his Black Little Eyes shining like beads in the moonlight, and she knew it was Trailer the Mink. She knew that Trailer was not coming on a friendly visit, because he had no friends among the Furry Folk. No, sir; Trailer was not friendly toward anyone.

No doubt Mrs. Muskrat could have dived right off her house into the water and escaped. She could easily have swum faster than Trailer, because her hind feet were broad and strong, and she

Mrs. Muskrat was busy making the walls of her bedroom.

could use her tail when she was swimming. If Mrs. Muskrat had dived under water, Trailer the Mink would not have seen which way she was swimming.

But Mrs. Muskrat did not choose to dive into the water. Oh, no! It was *her* Grassy House, and she would not be chased away. And, besides, she feared that Trailer might surprise Danny when he came back, and kill him. So Mrs. Muskrat sat up on her Grassy House, with her long, sharp teeth showing, and waited for Trailer to swim nearer. She was determined to fight it out with him. Mrs. Muskrat was angry, and when Trailer came near, she bit at him furiously.

"Don't you dare to come near my Grassy House," she squealed loudly.

Trailer the Mink was rather surprised. He had hoped that he could pounce on Mrs. Muskrat when she was not looking. But there she sat on her Grassy House waiting to spring on him the moment he came near enough. Then Trailer decided he would try to fool Mrs. Muskrat.

"Good evening," he said in his friendliest voice. "I noticed that you were building a new Grassy House, and I thought I would come over to see it."

Trailer thought that if he acted very friendly, Mrs. Muskrat would not watch him so closely.

"Don't you dare to come near my
Grassy House," squealed Mrs. Muskrat loudly.

Then he could pounce upon her when she was not looking. He thought if he could only get out of the water and onto her Grassy House he could spring better.

But Mrs. Muskrat was not so easily fooled. She did not trust Trailer the Mink, because she had heard many stories from her Furry Friends about how cruel Trailer was. Trailer was like some people, he had a very bad reputation. Sometimes there are people who do things that they should not do, and soon everyone knows about it. That was the way it was with Trailer the Mink.

"You stay away from my Grassy House!" squealed Mrs. Muskrat again, and she snapped her long, sharp teeth.

Now it happened that when Danny Muskrat started toward the edge of the Fuzzy Cattail Patch, he had not gone more than halfway until he found plenty of material with which to build his Grassy House. Yes, there was more Swamp Grass and Green Moss and other things than he needed. So Danny set to work gathering a large load of it to bring back with him.

When Danny had his load almost ready, he thought he heard Mrs. Muskrat squeal. Danny was quiet for a moment while he listened. Sure enough, in a moment he heard her squeal again. You should have seen Danny drop his load of Swamp Grass and start toward his Grassy House. My, how Danny did speed through the water! He went so fast he made Long Silvery Ripples that shot out on each side of him.

Soon Danny was close enough to see his Grassy House. There was Mrs. Muskrat sitting on top guarding it, while Trailer the Mink was wondering if he dared to climb up.

Danny speeded toward his Grassy House as fast as he could. He knew that Mrs. Muskrat was in trouble and needed his help. The first thing Trailer knew, he felt Danny's sharp teeth in his back, and he was pulled out of sight under the water. When he came up he saw Danny sitting on the Grassy House beside Mrs. Muskrat, and Trailer the Mink decided it was time for him to leave.

"Now maybe Trailer the Mink will leave us alone," said Danny Muskrat, when he saw Trailer hurrying away.

It was a sore Trailer that crawled into a Hiding Place to lick his wound as the Laughing Yellow Sun was peeping up over the Old Homestead. You see, Trailer's back hurt him so much that he could not even get back to his own Hidden Den.

CHAPTER 6

Paddletail Does Some Exploring

PADDLETAIL the Beaver had been living in a Hidden Den in a Clay Bank of his Wildwood Pond not far from where Danny Muskrat had been living. The doorway to his Hidden Den was under water as was Danny's, but his Hidden Den was much larger and higher.

"Let us build a Brushy House," said Paddletail one day to Mrs. Paddletail.

"I do believe it would be nicer," said Mrs. Paddletail; "but where shall we build it?"

"We will find a place," said Paddletail.

You see, when Paddletail had his High Dam repaired and the water in his Wildwood Pond was higher, it covered more ground, and it had reached back where there were many, many trees standing. Paddletail thought he could find a place where there were plenty of trees out of which he could build a Brushy House.

So away went Paddletail to find a nice place where he could build a Brushy House. Of course you know that Shaggy the Wolf had been waiting around for a chance to catch Paddletail while he

Shaggy saw Paddletail leave his High Dam.

was building a Secluded Ditch, but Paddletail had decided to build a Brushy House first.

When Paddletail started out to find a nice building place, he went to inspect his High Dam first. He wanted to be sure that it was all right, for sometimes the water found Tiny Little Openings, which it soon made larger, and then Paddletail had to fill them with Green Moss and Tangled Brush over which he plastered mud that he took from the Clay Bank.

Paddletail found that the High Dam was all right, and he swam away in search of a place to build a Brushy House. Paddletail really intended to build a Brushy House when he first made his High Dam and the Wildwood Pond. But he had not had time to build his High Dam as high as he wanted it that year before Old Man Winter started down from the Land of Ice. Paddletail thought he would build it higher some day, and he knew that if he built a Brushy House first, it would be under water when he raised his High Dam. So the Paddletails had made a Hidden Den in a Clay Bank where they could live until their High Dam was finished. That was why Paddletail was ready to build his Brushy House as soon as he found a place that suited him.

Shaggy the Wolf saw Paddletail leave his High Dam and start to swim around the Wildwood Pond.

"I do believe that Paddletail is going to finish his Secluded Ditch at last," said Shaggy to himself.

But Paddletail had decided he did not need a Secluded Ditch at that time. He had found that the High Dam had flooded many, many more trees, and he did not need a Secluded Ditch to get to them. Yes, sir; Shaggy the Wolf was mistaken.

Around the Wildwood Pond swam Paddletail, and all the time Shaggy was watching him. "Now what do you suppose Paddletail is looking for?" thought Shaggy.

After a while Paddletail came to a place that looked inviting. There was much Bitter Willow

Brush growing there, and not far away were many, many Soft Poplar Trees and Cottonwood Trees and other trees that Paddletail liked. They were growing on a Broad Flat, and Paddletail thought that he could make Secluded Ditches to them when he was ready to cut them.

"I believe I will get Mrs. Paddletail and see if she likes this place," said Paddletail, and away he went toward his Hidden Den.

Soon he was returning with Mrs. Paddletail, and not far behind were Brownie and Silver Paddletail.

"Oh, this is a fine place to build a Brushy House!" said Mrs. Paddletail, when she saw the spot that Paddletail had chosen.

"Yes, this is a very good place," the others agreed.

Sometimes Paddletail would stop long enough to play a game.

Then the Paddletails began to cut Bitter Willow Brush and Soft Poplar Trees, and in a little while they were carrying brush and sticks and even rocks and making a large pile. You see, Paddletail put rocks on the brush to hold it down in the water.

"Now I think the Paddletails are building a Brushy House," said Shaggy the Wolf. "I'll watch, and when Paddletail comes after a rock, I'll catch him."

So Shaggy the Wolf waited in the trees near the Wildwood Pond and watched for Paddletail when he would better have been away looking for something else to eat.

Brownie Paddletail and Silver were having a fine time. They ate the Tender Buds and Spicy Bark from the Soft Poplar Trees that Paddletail cut down, and then they played Dive.

Sometimes Paddletail would stop long enough to play a game also. It was a strange game called Spin. First Paddletail would sink head first in the water until his body was out of sight. Then he would whirl his tail swiftly around and around and make large Foam Circles in the water about him. No one could have seen anything but the end of his tail sticking out.

Paddletail's tail was large and flat like a canoe

paddle, and it helped him greatly when he was swimming. Some people thought that Paddletail used his broad tail as a trowel with which to plaster his Brushy House and High Dam, or on which to carry things, but that was not so. Paddletail carried his clay and rocks and sods and such things with his front feet, holding the load against his chest under his chin.

When the Weird Darkness was being chased away by Golden Streamers and it was almost time for the Laughing Yellow Sun to jump up, Paddletail and his family stopped work on their new Brushy House and swam back toward their Hidden Den.

"Well, I must wait until tomorrow night to catch Paddletail," said Shaggy the Wolf, and he licked his long, white fangs with his red tongue. Then he turned and ran into the Black Forest for an all-day sleep himself.

CHAPTER 7

Sticker the Porcupine Wins Out

SHAGGY the Wolf awoke as the Long Shadows were chasing one another through the Black Forest. "Yow-oooooo," he howled; "I certainly am hungry."

Shaggy had had nothing to eat the night before, and his stomach was empty. "I wonder if Paddletail will come out where I can catch him," thought he. "Perhaps I should try to catch Snowshoe."

But Shaggy had his mind set on catching Paddletail, and he started toward the Wildwood Pond, hoping that Paddletail would be at work on his new Brushy House.

Sure enough, when Shaggy arrived at the Wildwood Pond, he saw Paddletail and Mrs. Paddletail and the Young Paddletails near the new Brushy House. Paddletail was finishing cutting down a tree, and Brownie and Silver were playing.

Crash! went the tree, and splash! went the water. You see, the tree was standing in water where Paddletail had flooded the ground with his High Dam; but it was not under water far enough so that Paddletail had to work under water.

Lutra the Otter and his friends were playing a game of Slide.

As soon as the tree crashed down, Paddletail began to cut off the limbs so he could use them for his Brushy House. And Brownie and Silver Paddletail started to eat their breakfast of Tender Buds and Spicy Bark.

"We must finish this Brushy House tonight," said Mrs. Paddletail, as she helped to cut off some limbs.

"Yes, we have been working on it long enough," said Paddletail. "Let us finish it, and then we will not need to go back to the Hidden Den."

So they both worked as fast as they could to get the new Brushy House finished that night. And there was Shaggy the Wolf hiding in a Wild Plum Thicket and growing hungrier every minute.

Paddletail was bringing in about the last load, which would finish his Brushy House, when he heard a noise. Kerplunk, kerplunk, kerplunk, it sounded.

"That must be Lutra the Otter and his friends playing a game of Slide," said Paddletail.

Lutra the Otter and his friends lived in a Friendly Burrow among the spreading roots of a Giant Cottonwood that stood on the bank of Little River not far from the Duck Pond on the Old Homestead. Lutra was a near relative of Snoop the Weasel and Trailer the Mink and Killer the Marten. Besides catching many, many fish, Lutra liked to play Slide. He liked to go visiting, too, and sometimes he followed along Little River until it came to Paddletail's Wildwood Pond in the Black Forest. Whenever Lutra saw a nice Sloping Bank with a Quiet Pool at the bottom, he built a Mud Slide. And at Paddletail's Wildwood Pond he had built an extra long Mud Slide.

Lutra usually took some friends with him when he went visiting. Perhaps it was because he liked to play Slide with them. He would scoot down the Mud Slide on his stomach kerplunk into the water. His wet fur made the Mud Slide as slick as could be. Then right behind him would come his friends, kerplunk, kerplunk.

Lutra liked to visit Padletail's Wildwood Pond because there were plenty of fish in it. He also liked the extra long Mud Slide on the Clay Bank, and when he was tired of fishing he could play.

Paddletail listened, and in a little while again he heard kerplunk, kerplunk, kerplunk. "Yes, that is Lutra, I am sure," he said.

When Paddletail had finished his Brushy House, he went inside to look around. The doorway to his Brushy House was under water, like the one to Danny Muskrat's Grassy House. In

Sticker the Porcupine was out for a stroll.

fact, they looked alike except that Paddletail's was many, many times larger, and it was made of different things. But, then, Paddletail was much larger than Danny Muskrat, and he needed a larger home. Danny was about twice as large as Mr. Barn Rat, while Paddletail weighed fifty pounds.

"I believe I will go over to the Broad Flat and see if I can find something good to eat," said Paddletail. He had been working hard almost all night, and he was getting hungry.

Now Paddletail did not know that Shaggy the Wolf was hidden in a Wild Plum Thicket and was waiting for him to go to the Broad Flat so he could catch him. Paddletail did not know that, or he would have gone to the other side of his Wildwood Pond. So he swam around toward the Broad Flat.

Shaggy the Wolf had about given up waiting for Paddletail to come to the Broad Flat, when suddenly he saw a Shadowy Form moving slowly along the ground.

"Well, well, I do believe that Paddletail has come ashore at last," said Shaggy.

Nearer and nearer came the Shadowy Form. It was moving slowly through the Leafy Bushes that grew on the ground. Shaggy could wait no longer. He did not even wait to make sure that it was Paddletail. Out of the Wild Plum Thicket he raced and sprang at the Shadowy Form. "Yow-oooooo!" he howled, for all around his mouth there were Sharp Little Spears sticking deeply into the flesh and hurting dreadfully.

He did not notice that it was not Paddletail until it was too late to stop. That was one time when Shaggy the Wolf made a serious mistake, for it was not Paddletail at all but Sticker the Porcupine, who was out for a stroll.

Sticker the Porcupine carries many Sharp Little Spears on his back and tail; and when an enemy attacks him, it gets them into its mouth. That is what happened to Shaggy the Wolf, and Shaggy had a sore mouth for many a day.

CHAPTER 8

A Visit to the Broad Flat

WHEN Paddletail reached the Broad Flat, he did not go far from the water. No, sir; Paddletail was too wise for that. Besides Shaggy the Wolf and Ranger the Coyote, Paddletail had two other Furry Enemies. They were Growler the Bear and Carcajou the Glutton. Paddletail feared that if he went too far from his Wildwood Pond, one of them might come along and catch him. Of course he had other Furry Enemies also, but he did not fear them so much.

It did not take Paddletail long to find a tree that suited his taste, and soon he was dining on the Tender Buds and Spicy Bark of a Soft Poplar Tree.

"I believe I will take a large limb of this Soft Poplar Tree home with me for Mrs. Paddletail and the Youngsters," said Paddletail, and he bit off as large a limb as he could drag. Soon he was swimming toward his Brushy House, pulling the large limb after him.

"See what we are going to have for our dinner!" exclaimed Brownie Paddletail, when he saw Paddletail coming.

"Tomorrow night I will take you over to the Broad Flat," said Paddletail.

"Oh, that will be fun," said Silver Paddletail. "Then we can cut down some Slender Treelets ourselves."

While the Young Paddletails were eating, Paddletail and Mrs. Paddletail went into their Brushy House to do some work. Although Paddletail had all the work done on the outside of his home that was needed until Old Man Winter came along and made him plaster it tighter with Green Moss and Oozy Mud, still there was work to be done inside.

When Paddletail made the walls of his Brushy House, he laid the sticks crisscross and almost every way. Many of the ends were sticking inside his home for him to bump his head on. It would

Paddletail cut off all those troublesome sticks.

never do to leave them there for the Young Paddletails to run into, and, besides, the sticks took too much room.

So Paddletail had to go into his new Brushy House and cut off all those troublesome sticks to make the walls inside of his home nice and even. Then when Paddletail wanted to make his room larger, he cut the sticks off more.

Of course the Paddletails could not finish their Brushy House in one night. They would have to work on it many, many nights before it suited them. But then the the Paddletails had to be busy doing something. Perhaps that is one reason why they never got into trouble. They worked so much and played so much that they had no time to get into mischief.

Someone has said that Satan finds something for idle hands to do. That means that if we are idle, it gives Satan an opportunity to tempt us to do the things we should not do. So when the Paddletails were not playing Swim or Dive or Spin, they were busy fixing their Brushy House or their High Dam, or they were building Secluded Ditches.

One reason Paddletail promised to take the Young Paddletails to the Broad Flat was that he planned on making some Secluded Ditches there.

He knew that soon the Young Paddletails would be large enough to go to the Broad Flat alone; and he was afraid that if there were no Secluded Ditches for them to hide in, a Furry Enemy might catch them.

So the next night all the Paddletails started for the Broad Flat in the Weird Darkness. Paddletail did not like to work while the Smiling Moon was watching him. He would rather work during dark nights.

"Do not go far from the Wildwood Pond," said Paddletail to Brownie and Silver. "There are many Furry Enemies in the Black Forest, and they will catch you."

Then Paddletail and Mrs. Paddletail set to work on their Secluded Ditches. It was rather slow work for the Paddletails to dig their Secluded Ditches, for they had to take away the soil as fast as they dug it. Paddletail expected to work on his Secluded Ditches many, many nights. One of them was to be dug away back to a Quaking Aspen Grove where there were many Quaking Aspen Trees that the Paddletails liked.

At last Paddletail and Mrs. Paddletail stopped work for the night. They were hungry, and they thought they would eat some Tender Buds and Spicy Bark before going to their Brushy House.

The Paddletails set
to work on their
Secluded Ditches.

"Now where do you suppose those Youngsters are?" asked Mrs. Paddletail. "I can't see them anywhere."

"Perhaps they are in the Leafy Bushes along the bank," said Paddletail.

But although Paddletail and Mrs. Paddletail looked in the Leafy Bushes and along the shore of the Wildwood Pond, they could not find Brownie and Silver.

"Oh, dear, I wonder what could have happened to them!" said Mrs. Paddletail. "I do hope that they are not lost in the Black Forest, where Carcajou the Glutton might catch them."

Golden Streamers were shooting up in the east, which told the Paddletails that the Laughing Yellow Sun would soon be getting up.

"It looks as if we shall have to go back to the Brushy House without them," said Mrs. Paddletail.

Paddletail was hungry because he had been looking for Brownie and Silver instead of eating. So he cut off a large branch from a Soft Poplar Tree and took it with him to eat by his Brushy House. Mrs. Paddletail stopped to nibble a little herself, and then she dived down to the tunnel that led to the doorway of her Brushy House. In a moment she had swum through the tunnel and had come up again inside her home. Then what do you suppose Mrs. Paddletail saw? Why, Brownie and Silver, and both of them sound asleep.

CHAPTER 9

Lightfoot the Deer Comes for a Drink

SNEAK the Cougar lived in a cavelike opening in a Rocky Cliff in the Black Forest. Some people called Sneak a Panther, and others called him a Mountain Lion. He was even called a Catamount. Sneak the Cougar certainly had plenty of names, but his real name was Puma.

Sneak was a near relative of Shadow the Lynx and Hunting Cat. He belonged to the cat family. Some people said that Sneak the Cougar never screamed. Others said that he did. As a matter of fact, Sneak screamed sometimes; but he did not do it very often.

Sneak was a great tree climber. He liked to lie on a large branch of a tree near the ground; and when a deer passed under, down would spring Sneak onto its back. He would grab the deer's nose with his sharp claws and twist its head. In that way he would break its neck.

Although Sneak was a terrible killer of Furred and Feathered Creatures, he was afraid of Fearful the Man. People told stories of how Sneak had killed and eaten human beings, but almost all these stories were not true. Sneak was large enough and strong enough to kill an unarmed man if he wished, but he was a coward.

Sometimes when Terror the Hunter was out stalking game, Sneak followed along behind him out of sight; but he never had courage to pounce upon him unawares.

Sneak surely did like to hunt for Lightfoot the Deer. Lightfoot lived in the Black Forest, and most of the time he hid among the Leafy Bushes.

One day Lightfoot the Dear saw Shaggy the Wolf chasing Molly Cottontail. You see, Molly had come over to the Big Jungle Thicket in the Black Forest to look for Peter, and Shaggy the Wolf had seen her.

When Lightfoot saw Shaggy chasing Molly, he ran as fast as his trim legs would carry him, and hid in a Dense Cedar Thicket. He was afraid that Shaggy might chase him. "I believe I shall be safe if I stop here to rest," he said.

But Lightfoot had been seen by other eyes. Sneak the Cougar had been lying on a Rocky Ledge in the warm sunshine, watching for something to stalk. When he saw Lightfoot stop in the Dense Cedar Thicket, he bared his needlelike claws and waved his long tail as Hunting Cat did when he was contented. Then he left his Rocky

Ledge and sneaked silently in the direction of the Dense Cedar Thicket.

Sneak the Cougar knew that he never could get near enough to Lightfoot to pounce upon him while he was in the Dense Cedar Thicket. Lightfoot had a sensitive nose, a keen nose indeed. When he stopped in the Dense Cedar Thicket he was careful to stay on the opposite side from which the Playful Air Whiffs were coming. Then if Sneak the Cougar tried to catch him, he could smell Sneak coming. If Sneak tried to approach against the Playful Air Whiffs, Lightfoot was where he could see him.

Sneak the Cougar was wise enough to know this. He knew that he could not catch Lightfoot napping. He also knew that after Lightfoot had rested, he would come out from the Dense Cedar Thicket for a drink at Paddletail's Wildwood Pond. Sneak thought that then would be a good time to catch Lightfoot. So he crawled out on a Big Limb near the Wildwood Pond and waited.

Sure enough, out came Lightfoot as the Long Shadows were beginning to chase one another through the Black Forest. What is more, Lightfoot started to walk right toward the place where Sneak was waiting. Snip, snip, went Lightfoot, as he pulled some Savory Twigs from the Leafy

Bushes. Then he walked a little closer to Sneak.

Sneak flattened out on the Big Limb and made ready to spring when Lightfoot came near enough. Snip, snip, and Lightfoot pulled off another bite of Savory Twigs. In a little while Lightfoot would be near enough for Sneak to spring on to him.

Suddenly there was a loud whack on the water not far away. Then Lightfoot snorted, and ran from there as fast as he could with his funny stiff-legged jumps.

You see, Paddletail the Beaver was going to the Broad Flat to start his night's work on his Secluded Ditches. He had been swimming near the bank, when he spied Sneak the Cougar up on the Big Limb. Whenever Paddletail knew that there

"Snip, snip," and Lightfoot pulled off
another bite of Savory Twigs.

Sneak was waiting to pounce on Lightfoot.

was danger near, he believed in warning all the other Wild Creatures around him. So he always slapped the water loudly with his broad tail before he dived out of sight.

Paddletail did not know that Sneak the Cougar was waiting to pounce on Lightfoot the Deer. Paddletail did not know that. But he knew that Sneak was up to some mischief. If Paddletail had gone under the Big Limb, Sneak would as soon have jumped down upon him; and Paddletail knew it.

Lightfoot the Deer never knew that Paddletail had saved his life. Sometimes we do a good turn for a friend and he never knows it; but that is the best way to do good. Sometimes we help a friend

(61)

and we do not know it ourselves. That was the way it was with Paddletail; but it surely did upset Sneak's plans.

When Paddletail came up again, he was far from the place where he had seen Sneak.

"I guess Sneak will not bother anyone for a while," he said, as he swam toward the Broad Flat. Soon he was busy digging away at his Secluded Ditches.

There sat Peter Cottontail watching Paddletail cut down a tree.

CHAPTER 10

Snowshoe the Hare Is Frightened

SNOWSHOE the Hare lived in a Willow Thicket that was along Little River above where it flowed into Paddletail's Wildwood Pond in the Black Forest. Snowshoe was a near relative of Molly and Peter Cottontail. He was also a cousin of Jack the Jumper, but he was different from both the Cottontails and Jack the Jumper.

You see, Molly and Peter lived in a Friendly Burrow in the Little Jungle Thicket on the Old Homestead, but Snowshoe the Hare never lived in a Friendly Burrow. He lived in a Cozy Form in the Willow Thicket. He was about twice as large as the Cottontails, and he had large hind feet, which helped him to run across the Fleecy Snow in the wintertime without sinking in deeply. When Old Man Winter came, Snowshoe took off his brownish coat and put on a white one so that Great Horn the Owl and Shadow the Lynx could not see him so easily when he was sitting on the Fleecy Snow.

Snowshoe looked more like his cousin Jack the Jumper than he looked like the Cottontails, but he was much smaller than Jack. Jack liked to stay in the Wide-Wide Pasture and the Open Fields instead of in the Black Forest as Snowshoe did. Neither Jack nor the Cottontails wore white coats in winter.

While Snowshoe was like his relatives in some ways, in other ways he was not. That is the way it is with us. Sometimes we look like our relatives, but we do not always like the things they like or do the things they do.

Snowshoe the Hare had a Great Enemy. Of course he had many enemies, but none were so dreaded as the Great Enemy. That was Shadow the Lynx. Shadow the Lynx also had large, padded feet on which he could follow Snowshoe silently over Fleecy Snow without any trouble. And Shadow the Lynx certainly did like to hunt Snowshoe. Winter and summer he was always sneaking through the Willow Thickets and Brushy Hillsides as silent as a shadow, while he looked for something to pounce upon, and especially for Snowshoe.

Shadow the Lynx was a relative of Sneak the Cougar, and he was fully as bloodthirsty. He wore a grizzled coat something like Sneak's, but he did not have a long tail such as Hunting Cat and Sneak the Cougar had. It was only a stub. But,

Snowshoe had large
hind feet.

then, Shadow wore a fancy tassel on the top of
each ear, which his relatives had not, and that
made up for the lack of tail.

One day Snowshoe the Hare was resting in the
Big Jungle Thicket. He had gone to the Big
Jungle Thicket for the same reason that his cousin
Peter had gone there. He thought he would find
Tender Green Things to eat. Snowshoe had built
himself a Cozy Form, and was resting. In fact,
Snowshoe was sound asleep. He was wearing his
brownish summer coat, and it was the color of the
Brown Leaflets and Dry Sticks and Dead Grass
that he had used to make his form of. Snowshoe
felt quite safe, for he thought no one would see
him. So he had gone sound asleep.

Suddenly there was a loud noise that scared

Snowshoe half out of his wits. "Brrrrrrruuuuuuuu-nnnnnmm!" went the noise near where Snowshoe was sleeping. He awakened so suddenly that for a moment he could not tell where he was or which way to run. Then Snowshoe saw Drummer the Grouse sitting on his Favorite Drumming Log and smoothing his feathers.

"My, how you frightened me!" exclaimed Snowshoe the Hare. "I thought surely that Shadow the Lynx had jumped for me through the brush."

Drummer the Grouse finished smoothing his feathers and said nothing. Then he braced his feet, moved his wings slowly back and forth as if to be sure there was plenty of room, and soon they were

"My, how you frightened me!" exclaimed
Snowshoe to Drummer.

beating the air so swiftly they were one blur.

"Brrrrrrruuuuuuuunnnnnnmm!" went Drummer the Grouse. Then he started right in to smooth his feathers all over again.

"Vain bird," thought Snowshoe, and he hopped out of his Cozy Form and started toward his own Willow Thicket. No doubt Snowshoe thought he would go where there was not so much noise to keep him awake.

That was a lucky move for Snowshoe, for Snowshoe was not the only one who had heard Drummer the Grouse. Over in a Blue Spruce Thicket Shadow the Lynx had been hiding and waiting for Snowshoe to pass by so he could pounce upon him. Shadow heard Drummer the Grouse, and it gave him an idea.

"I believe I will sneak over and catch Drummer the Grouse when he is not looking," said Shadow the Lynx. Away he went through the Leafy Bushes in the direction that he had heard Drummer.

Now it happened that when Drummer first awoke Snowshoe the Hare with his loud noise, Reddy Fox was slipping through the tall grass that grew along the edge of the Black Forest. He was looking for Tiny the Meadow Mouse or Hungarian the Partridge or Dodger the Gopher or almost anything that suited his taste. He had been hunting a long time without finding anything, and he was hungry.

"Aha," said Reddy Fox, when he heard Drummer the Grouse; "I hear Drummer on his Favorite Drumming Log. I will slip over and catch him when he isn't looking."

So while Shadow the Lynx was sneaking over to catch Drummer the Grouse, there was Reddy Fox starting out also. Yes sir; it was a lucky move for Snowshoe the Hare when he left and went back to his own Willow Thicket.

CHAPTER 11

Drummer Has a Narrow Escape

THERE is no doubt that Drummer the Grouse was a vain bird, as Snowshoe the Hare had said, although he had no reason at all for being vain. He was really quite common-looking in his gray checked suit when compared with the beautiful colored uniform that Ringneck the Pheasant wore. Ringneck the Pheasant flapped his wings and crowed sometimes; but he never made a big noise as if he were showing off, as Drummer did.

Now it may be that Drummer was not trying to show off, but it certainly looked like it. Perhaps he was a musician and enjoyed drumming on his Favorite Drumming Log.

It seems as if Drummer should have known better than to make so much noise and let all his Furry Enemies know where he was. But there he was, going "Brrrrrrruuuuuuunnnnnnmm!" every little while, while Reddy Fox and Shadow the Lynx were both sneaking over to pounce on him. He might as well have said: "Here I am. Come and get me."

Shadow the Lynx was not in any hurry to get to Drummer. Oh, no! He sneaked around through the Leafy Bushes and over Rocky Ledges. He thought he might find Snowshoe along the way. He even went along the Marshy Bank of Paddletail's Wildwood Pond to see if Jimmy the Swamp Rabbit was there. He thought he surely ought to meet someone.

Jimmy the Swamp Rabbit was another cousin of Snowshoe, but he looked more like Molly and Peter Cottontail. Jimmy did not mind swimming at all. If Snoop the Weasel or Trailer the Mink or some other Furry Enemy came after him, he would jump right into the water and swim away from them.

But Snowshoe was not like that. He did not like to swim. Once when he was caught in a Foaming Flood, he jumped up on a stump, and there he sat until he almost starved to death rather than jump off and swim over where he could get something to eat.

Shadow the Lynx explored the Marshy Bank and then went over to the Wild Plum Thicket where Shaggy the Wolf sometimes hid. And all the time he was getting closer to the Big Jungle Thicket where Drummer the Grouse was making a noise that sounded as if someone were pounding on the bottom of an empty barrel. Of course if Shadow the Lynx had known that Reddy Fox was on his way to find Drummer, he would have been in more of a hurry; but Shadow did not know that.

Neither did Reddy Fox know that Shadow was planning on catching Drummer, or he would not have spent so much time looking for Tiny the Meadow Mouse along the way.

You see, Reddy Fox liked to sniff into every little Friendly Burrow and bunch of Tangled Grasses that he saw. He thought that he might scare out Tiny, or Tiny's cousin, Whitefoot the Mouse. Reddy Fox belonged to the same family as Shaggy the Wolf and Ranger the Coyote, but he did not hunt as they did. He hunted more like

Shadow the Lynx was not in a hurry.

Shadow the Lynx, by stalking, while Shaggy and Ranger preferred to outrun their victims.

"Brrrrrrruuuuuuuunnnnnnmm!" went Drummer the Grouse again.

Reddy Fox was not far away. "My, but won't grouse taste good!" he thought.

Then Reddy came to the edge of the Big Jungle Thicket and began to crawl through the Wild Berry Bushes and Live Oak Brush and Twining Vines. "Sniff, sniff," he went, and the Playful Air Whiffs told him that Drummer the Grouse was not far away. Reddy was careful not to make a noise. He knew that if he stepped on Dry Sticks the noise would warn Drummer.

On the other side of the Big Jungle Thicket was Shadow the Lynx starting in. His soft, padded feet carried him along as silently as Great Horn the Owl could have flown. Everywhere that Shadow went, there were many, many Sheltered Bunny Lanes where Peter and Snowshoe and their friends had been playing. Shadow walked carefully, because he thought he might surprise one of them sitting behind a Leafy Bush.

Suddenly he heard Drummer the Grouse boom out again, and Shadow knew that he was almost there. He slipped around through the Leafy Bushes until he came to a Little Open Space, and

Reddy Fox bared his sharp, white teeth and barked angrily.

right there before his eyes sat Drummer on his Favorite Drumming Log, smoothing his feathers.

Now it happened that Reddy Fox was sitting behind a Leafy Bush not far away, ready to spring at Drummer, when Shadow the Lynx came near, with his eyes also on Drummer.

"Sniff, sniff," went Reddy; "I smell Shadow the Lynx. I must hurry and catch Drummer before Shadow gets him."

Out sprang Reddy Fox from behind his Leafy Bush in time to meet Shadow the Lynx face to face.

"Psst, psst!" hissed Shadow; "what business have you here?"

Reddy Fox bared his sharp, white teeth and barked angrily; and away flew Drummer the Grouse.

(73)

"Now see what you have done!" said Reddy Fox.

"You did it yourself," spat Shadow; "you should have stayed away."

"As if you owned the Big Jungle Thicket!" replied Reddy. "Why didn't you stay away yourself?"

"Haw haw haw," laughed someone overhead; and when Reddy Fox and Shadow the Lynx looked up, they saw Tattler the Jay sitting on a limb.

"Haw haw haw," he laughed; "that was so funny."

Shadow the Lynx and Reddy Fox felt cheap, and so they slipped away in opposite directions among the Wild Berry Bushes and Live Oak Brush and Twining Vines.

"Haw haw haw," laughed Tattler the Jay, and away he flew to see what mischief he could find to get into.

CHAPTER 12

Paddletail Has a Near Neighbor

DANDY the Chickadee seemed to be a carefree bird. It seemed as if all he had to do was to flit about from morning till night among the Quaking Aspens and other trees, looking for Tree Borers and Crawly Bark Lice to eat.

Dandy's home was in a hole in an Old Stump on the Broad Flat near the Wildwood Pond. At least that was where Mrs. Chickadee had her nest. But Dandy spent most of his time playing among the trees, sometimes hanging from the bottom of branches while he looked along the bottom side for Crawly Bark Lice and other things.

Dandy the Chickadee was Whitebreast the Nuthatch's cousin, and sometimes they ran races to see who could find the most good things. Of course Whitebreast the Nuthatch usually won, because he could run right down the side of a tree headfirst when he wanted to. When he was sitting on the side of a tree, he did not need to prop himself up with his tail as Redhead the Woodpecker and Judge Flicker did. He could hang on with his toes and go up or down or sideways.

Dandy stopped in
Crooner's tree for
a visit.

Dandy the Chickadee must have been proud
of his name, for he kept repeating it over and
over. "Chickadee-dee-dee, Chickadee-dee-dee," is
what he said while he flitted from tree to tree or
hung from the bottom of a limb. Dandy really was
a good-looking bird in his black cap and white
waistcoat and black bow tie. He was a pert-look-
ing bird indeed. But Dandy was not the only one
who could hang from the bottom of a limb; Timid
the Kinglet could do as well.

Not far from Dandy's home in the Old Stump
was the nest of Crooner the Dove. Crooner's nest
was in the Springy Branches of a Giant Cottonwood Tree that grew on the Broad Flat. Crooner
the Dove and Dandy the Chickadee were good
friends.

One day when Dandy came home after exploring the Quaking Aspen Grove, he found Crooner in trouble. Dandy stopped in Crooner's tree for a visit, and there sat Crooner making Mournful Noises.

"What is the matter?" asked Dandy, as he clung saucily from a limb. Whenever we are in trouble, we are glad to see a friend, you know, and so Crooner felt better when he saw Dandy.

"Hooknose the Chicken Hawk is building a nest in the top of that Soft Poplar Tree," said Crooner, "and I don't dare to go any place, or he will catch me."

Dandy the Chickadee looked over at the Soft Poplar Tree. It was near Crooner's Giant Cottonwood Tree on the Broad Flat and not far from one of Paddletail's Secluded Ditches.

Of course neither Dandy the Chickadee nor Crooner the Dove wanted Hooknose the Chicken Hawk for a near neighbor. They would not know what minute he would swoop down and carry them away.

Hooknose the Chicken Hawk and Sharpshin the Hawk were cousins, but Hooknose was much the larger. Of course if he could catch plenty of Farmer Smith's chickens, or some of Bobby White's family, or the friends of Ringneck the

Pheasant or Hungarian the Partridge, he did not bother with little birds like Dandy the Chickadee. But he might take a notion to kill Crooner the Dove.

So Crooner the Dove and Dandy the Chickadee began to plan how they could get rid of Hooknose. Sometimes we have neighbors who are not the kind we want, and we wish that they would move. We should first try to do all we can to help them; but, of course, like some neighbors, Hooknose was past being helped.

"Now, how can we get rid of Hooknose?" asked Crooner the Dove.

"It would serve him right if Terror the Hunter came along with his gun," said Dandy. "He has no business here by the Wildwood Pond."

"No, he hasn't," said Crooner. "There will be no peace if he is near. But I don't see how we can get rid of him."

Dandy was thoughtful for a moment. The Laughing Yellow Sun was ready to bow out of sight in the Golden West, and Paddletail the Beaver came out of his Brushy House and swam toward the Secluded Ditch that he was making on the Broad Flat.

"Perhaps Paddletail can help us," said Dandy the Chickadee. "I'll fly over and ask him." So

Dandy flew to the place where Paddletail would soon be digging.

"Good evening," said Dandy.

"Good evening," replied Paddletail, for he was glad to see Dandy.

You see, Dandy and Paddletail were real good friends. Dandy the Chickadee and his cousin Whitebreast did not go to the Sunny Southland every winter as did most of Paddletail's Feathered Friends. No, sir; they stayed right there in the Black Forest all winter and hunted Tree Borers and such things. So Paddletail liked Dandy the Chickadee because he was a good neighbor all the year.

"I wonder if you could help Crooner the Dove and me out of trouble," said Dandy, and he cocked his head thoughtfully on one side.

Like some neighbors, Hooknose the Chicken Hawk was past being helped.

"What is the matter?" asked Paddletail.

"Hooknose the Chicken Hawk is building a nest in that Soft Poplar Tree by your Secluded Ditch, and there will be no peace at the Wildwood Pond while he is around."

"Well, well, he has his nerve!" said Paddletail. "It will never do for him to live there."

"But I do not see how we can get rid of him," said Dandy.

Paddletail thought for a moment while he nibbled the Spicy Bark from a piece of Soft Poplar Wood. And then Paddletail chuckled.

"I can make Hooknose leave," said Paddletail. "Yes, I can make him go away."

"I hope you can," said Dandy, as he flew away to his home in the Old Stump. It was getting dark, and Mrs. Chickadee would be wondering where he was.

Chapter 13

Ouzel the Dipper Plays Duck

AFTER Dandy the Chickadee left, Paddletail the Beaver swam up his Secluded Ditch until he was across from the Soft Poplar Tree where Hooknose the Chicken Hawk had started to build a nest. Then Paddletail left the Secluded Ditch and walked over to the Soft Poplar Tree.

"Yes, sir," chuckled Paddletail to himself: "I can stop Hooknose's nest building around here."

Then Paddletail set to work to cut down the Soft Poplar Tree. Of course he could not cut it entirely down in one night, because it was too large. And when Dandy the Chickadee came back the next morning for a visit with Crooner the Dove, there was Hooknose going right on building a nest.

"Oh, I do wish that Paddletail would help us!" said Crooner.

"He will, I know he will, because last night he said he would," said Dandy.

Suddenly Dandy noticed the chips on the ground around the Soft Poplar Tree.

"Oh, see those chips!" he said. "Paddletail has

Ouzel the Dipper
was a strange bird.

started to cut down the big Soft Poplar Tree."

That night when Crooner the Dove and Dandy the Chickadee were fast asleep, there was a loud crash. It fairly shook the ground. And the next morning, when it was light, they saw the Soft Poplar Tree lying on the ground.

"I am so glad," cooed Crooner. "Now Hooknose will have to look for another tree somewhere else if he doesn't want Paddletail to cut it down."

That is what Paddletail thought.

Besides Dandy the Chickadee and Whitebreast the Nuthatch, Paddletail had another neighbor that lived near him all winter. At least he was near him most of the winter. That was Ouzel the Dipper. That is a strange name for a bird but Ouzel was a strange bird. No one who saw Ouzel

would have believed that he could do the things
he did.

Ouzel lived right by Paddletail's High Dam,
and when Paddletail made his High Dam higher,
that suited Ouzel the Dipper.

To begin with, Ouzel looked something like
Jenny Wren, except that Ouzel was larger. But
when it came to doing tricks in the water, he was
fully as clever as Paddletail. No water was too
cold or too swift to stop Ouzel. He would sit on a
rock, or on the ice if it was winter, and suddenly
he would dive headfirst right into the water. Sometimes he would dive through the Swift Waterfall
that was falling over Paddletail's High Dam, and
walk along back of it. Then again he would walk
along on the bottom of a Quiet Pool. But the place
that Ouzel the Dipper liked best was near Paddletail's Swift Waterfall.

Have you ever played the game of Pretend? Of
course you have. Everyone has played that. When
I was a boy I would sometimes pretend that I was
a storekeeper. Then all the playmates would come
to my store and pretend that they were buying all
kinds of things. Sometimes they would pretend
they were ill. Then I would pretend I was a doc-
tor, and I would give them spoonfuls of water or
something, which we pretended was medicine.

out to teach them how to catch fish. At first he caught the fish himself and stunned them so they would be easier for the Young Kingfishers to pick up out of the water. What a splash the Young Kingfishers made for a while until they learned to fly better! Then Alcyon let them catch their own fish.

CHAPTER 14

Mew-Mew the Catbird Plays a Joke

THE Thrashers and the Catbirds were real close neighbors, but that was not strange, for they were near relatives. Browny Thrasher and Mew-Mew the Catbird and Jenny Wren and Mr. Mockingbird all belonged to the same family. Jenny Wren liked to live in the eaves of the Grand Old House, where Judge Flicker had made her a doorway by pecking out a knot, and Mr. Mockingbird lived mostly in the Sunny Southland. So Browny Thrasher and Mew-Mew the Catbird were about the only ones of their relations who lived in the Black Forest.

"I do wish that Tattler the Jay would stay away from here," said Browny Thrasher one day. "He is always snooping around and waiting for a chance to get into mischief."

"Yes, I wish he would," said Mew-Mew; "but I don't know how we can keep him away."

"I hardly dare to hunt food for my babies while Tattler is around, because if he had a chance he would steal them," said Browny.

Anyone could have seen that Browny Thrasher

was worried, because he never sang any more. Browny really was an expert singer. He could sing almost as well as his cousin Mr. Mockingbird, and everyone knew that *he* could sing almost any tune that all the other Feathered Friends could sing. Yes, sir, Mr. Mockingbird could sing almost any tune, and so could Browny. But Browny was so worried about his babies that he had stopped singing.

Tattler the Jay certainly did make a nuisance of himself. He was a regular pest. It seemed as if all he had to do from morning until night was to fly through the Black Forest or around the Grand Old House or over to the Duck Pond, and pester other folks. He was a busybody. He was like some peo-

Browny Thrasher was so worried that he had stopped singing.

ple who can find time to meddle in other folks'
affairs instead of attending to their own business.
He was never welcome anywhere he went.

One day Tattler the Jay even went over to the
Grand Old House and tried to steal Robin Red's
babies while Robin Red and Mrs. Robin were
away. Tattler tried to take them out of the Red
Cedar in the yard. But Jenny Wren saw him and
yelled, "Thief, thief; robber, robber!" as loud as
she could, and Mr. Bluebird left his Nesting Box
near Robin Red's Red Cedar and flew and told
Mrs. Robin. You may be sure that Tattler the Jay
was glad to fly back to the Black Forest when
Robin Red and Mrs. Robin both got after him.

There he was waiting to steal Browny's babies
or Mew-Mew's babies if he had a chance.

Browny Thrasher and Mew-Mew the Catbird
had built nests real close together among the Blackberry Brambles and Tangled Brush and Twining
Vines in the Big Jungle Thicket. They were fond
of the Wild Berries that grew in the Big Jungle
Thicket. Their nests were well hidden among
the Dancing Leaflets; but nothing was safe from
the prying eyes of Tattler the Jay, and they all
knew it.

One day Tattler was slipping around through
the Big Jungle Thicket looking, as usual, for some-

thing to do. He had visited Crooner the Dove and had found him at home, so there was no chance for him to raid Crooner's nest. He could not get into Dandy the Chicadee's nest because it was in a hole in the Old Stump. Perhaps that was why Dandy had made it there. So Tattler the Jay had gone over to the Big Jungle Thicket to see if he could find the nests of Browny Thrasher or Mew-Mew the Catbird.

Now it happened that when Tattler arrived at the Big Jungle Thicket, the Thrashers were away looking for food for the Young Thrashers, and Mrs. Catbird was away also. Mew-Mew was hidden among the Leafy Bushes watching for Prowling Enemies, when there came Tattler the Jay hopping from bush to bush looking for Round Little Nests.

Mew-Mew knew that he was no match for Tattler alone. "Oh, dear, what shall I do?" he asked himself. "I do wish that Browny would return."

But Browny did not come back, and neither did Mrs. Thrasher nor Mrs. Catbird. And there was Tattler getting closer to the Round Little Nests every minute.

At last Tattler's sharp eyes spied Mew-Mew's Hungry Little Babies sticking their Wide-Mouths out of the Round Little Nest. They thought that

Mew-Mew was hiding among the Leafy Bushes
when Tattler the Jay came by.

Mew-Mew or Mrs. Catbird was bringing them a Fat Bug to eat.

"What luck!" thought Tattler the Jay. "There are the Baby Catbirds, and there is no one at home."

So he hopped down by the Round Little Nest, and was all ready to grab one of Mew-Mew's babies. "Oh, dear, I wish Browny would come," thought Mew-Mew; "but I must do something."

Then Mew-Mew thought of a scheme. Quietly he flew to a Leafy Bush right close to where Tattler the Jay was sitting. "Meow, meow," said Mew-Mew.

Tattler was so surprised that he did not stop to look around. No, sir; he did not wait to see where that noise came from. He flew to the top of a Great Pine Tree and scolded loudly.

"Now what do you suppose Hunting Cat is doing in the Black Forest?" he said to himself.

Of course Hunting Cat was not there at all. Mew-Mew had been playing the game of Pretend, and had fooled Tattler. But then Mew-Mew was not the only one among his relatives who liked to play Pretend. Sometimes Brown Thrasher pretended that he was one kind of bird, and sometimes he would sing like another. But Mr. Mockingbird was even better at making noises and singing like other birds. Perhaps Mew-Mew the Catbird thought it was better to make a noise like Hunting Cat, for then he could fool his Feathered Enemies. Did you ever hear Mew-Mew practicing how to do it? The next time you are in the Wildwood or near a Jungle Thicket, if you will listen closely, you will probably hear, "Meow, meow," and you will know that Mew-Mew is not far away.

CHAPTER 15

Carcajou the Glutton Goes Hunting

"HAVE you heard the news?" asked Snow-shoe the Hare, when he met Drummer the Grouse one day.

"No, what is it?" said Drummer.

"Carcajou the Glutton has come to the Black Forest," said Snowshoe; "and he is in a ferocious mood."

"Have you heard that Carcajou the Glutton is in the Black Forest?" asked Drummer of Light-foot the Deer, when he saw him.

"No, I did not know it," said Lightfoot.

"Well, he is, and he is as furious as usual."

"Carcajou the Glutton is hunting in the Black Forest," said Lightfoot the Deer to Paddletail the Beaver, when he went to Paddletail's Wildwood Pond for a drink.

Then Paddletail told Mrs. Paddletail and Brownie and Silver, and they told Danny Musk-rat, and Danny Muskrat told Dandy the Chick-adee, and Dandy told everyone he saw when he was flitting through the Black Forest looking for Tree Borers and Crawly Bark Lice.

(93)

Carcajou was feared
most by the little
Wild Creatures.

In a little while everyone in the Black Forest was telling everyone else: "Look out, Carcajou the Glutton is here."

Among all the Furry Enemies that ever came to the Black Forest, Carcajou the Glutton was feared the most by the little Wild Creatures. Yes, sir; there was none so dreaded as Carcajou. Sometimes he was called Wolverine the Terrible.

You see, Carcajou's home was in the Big Mountains, where Cervus the Elk lived. But sometimes he went hunting in the Black Forest, and then it was time for everyone to pass along a word of warning: "Look out, Carcajou the Glutton is here."

All along Little River and around the Duck Pond and through the little Jungle Thicket, where Molly and Peter lived, and even at the Grand Old

House and the Apple Orchard, everyone knew about it. They knew that Carcajou was in the Black Forest hunting, and they had better stay away.

It is little wonder that Carcajou the Glutton was so greatly feared by all the little Wild Creatures, because he was the largest and most bloodthirsty of a large family of murderers. Digger the Badger and Mephitis the Skunk and Killer the Marten and Fisher the Bold and Trailer the Mink and Lutra the Otter and Snoop the Weasel and Carcajou the Glutton all belong to the Weasel family.

Carcajou the Glutton was the largest and Snoop the Weasel was the smallest of this family. If you know how bloodthirsty Snoop the Weasel is, then you will know how ferocious Carcajou the Glutton was, for he was many, many times larger. He was almost as large as Nero the Hound, but his legs were much shorter and more powerful. In fact, Carcajou looked somewhat like a small bear. He had strong legs and very long, sharp claws, and with them he could tear apart Warm Hollow Logs after Bunnies, or dig out the Friendly Burrows of Furry Creatures, or rend apart Paddletail's Brushy House, unless it was frozen solid. And Carcajou had a terrible temper.

Now it happened that when Carcajou started out, almost the first one he met was Growler the Bear. Growler had found the carcass of an animal that a Hot Lightning Flash had killed, and he was having a feast.

Growler the Bear had been asleep during all the past winter. He had slept several months. When Jolly Spring awoke him, he felt hungry. His stomach had shrunk while he was asleep, because he had eaten nothing, and when he awoke it was not in condition to take much food. Anyway, Growler's feet had grown tender while he was not using them, and he could not walk far in search of food. They were cracked on the bottom and were peeling off. So Growler did not feel like using them much for a while. He did not care to dig after Tawny Chipmunk and Miner the Mole, and Tiny the Meadow Mouse.

So Growler had eaten some grass and twigs and dried berries for a while, whenever he could find some dried berries that the Feathered Friends had not eaten during the winter. He ate these things because they were handy and because they were what his lazy stomach needed to start it to work.

Growler had been awake two months now, and he was ready to eat almost anything he found.

When Carcajou saw Growler the Bear enjoying a feast, that was too much of a temptation for him.

"I'll go right over there and help myself," he grumbled, and away he went as fast as his short legs would carry him.

Of course, Carcajou should have had better manners than to interrupt Growler the Bear while he was eating. Anyone should have known better than that; but if Carcajou knew better, he did not care. No, sir; he went right up to that carcass and started to eat as if he had a perfect right to.

"You leave this alone!" growled Mr. Bear, and he chased Carcajou away; "this is my feast."

But Carcajou had had a taste of Growler's feast, and he wanted more. He thought he would grab a piece and run with it. So back he came and grabbed a leg right from under Growler's nose.

That was too much for Growler to stand, and he gave Carcajou a swift cuff that sent him rolling over and over. It was a wonder that Growler's strong claws had not torn Carcajou's coat wide open, even though it was very tough. But Carcajou escaped with some deep scratches, and he was glad to leave Growler's feast alone after that.

That was why Carcajou was in such a furious temper when he went to the Black Forest hunting.

CHAPTER 16

Mephitis the Skunk Takes a Stroll

IT may be that Growler the Bear was rather selfish in not giving Carcajou the Glutton part of his feast. But then Carcajou hardly deserved anything. He needed a lesson in manners; and that is what Growler gave him.

Of course Growler could not eat all his feast at one meal. What he expected to do was to eat his fill and then go to a Hiding Place and take a nap. Then when he was hungry again, he would come back for another feast. That was why he did not want Carcajou the Glutton to eat any of his food.

"Now I guess Mr. Glutton will leave my feast alone," said Growler the Bear, after Carcajou had left. And he did leave it alone, too.

My, how angry Carcajou was, though! Yes, sir, he was furious. It was no wonder that all the little Wild Creatures in the Black Forest were warning one another. Pesty the Magpie was the first to know about it. He had been helping himself to Growler's feast when Carcajou had come along, and Pesty had seen Growler cuff Carcajou end over end. Pesty had told Snowshoe the Hare

about it, and Snowshoe had told Drummer the
Grouse, and soon all the little Wild Creatures in
the Black Forest knew that Carcajou was there.
How they feared him!

"I do hope that Carcajou does not come to the
Wildwood Pond," said Paddletail the Beaver.

You see, Paddletail was afraid that Carcajou
would tear his Brushy House to pieces and catch
Brownie or Silver Paddletail. If only it had been
winter, then Carcajou could not tear the Brushy
House open while the walls were frozen solid.
But it wasn't, and, what was more, Paddletail's
Brushy House was new, and it was not so strong
as it would be after he had finished it for winter.
So Paddletail was worried.

Pesty had seen Growler cuff Carcajou.

Paddletail and the other little Wild Creatures were not the only ones that were worried about Carcajou sometimes. I should say not! Sometimes in the winter, when Trapper Jim had many, many traps set for Shaggy the Wolf and Reddy Fox and Ranger the Coyote and Killer the Marten, Carcajou would find Trapper Jim's tracks, and along he would follow behind Trapper Jim, out of sight, and he would steal the baits and spoil the sets; and if he found anything in the traps that Trapper Jim had caught, he would take that, too.

Once Carcajou the Glutton even broke into Trapper Jim's Cabin and ate most of his food. What he did not eat he scattered around and spoiled, and some of it he carried away with him. Carcajou was not only a murderer, but he was also a thief.

Trapper Jim disliked Carcajou as much as the little Wild Creatures did. He set traps to catch him, but Carcajou was too smart to be taken. Only once did he blunder into one of Trapper Jim's traps, and then Carcajou soon got out. Yes, sir; he pulled that trap apart with his strong legs, and away he went. It was no wonder that the Paddletails were worried when they heard that Carcajou was hunting in the Black Forest.

"I wonder what we should do," said Mr. Pad-

Down through the Green Meadow went Mephitis.

dletail. "I know that Carcajou will come right here and kill our babies."

Then he had an idea. "I know what we can do," he said; "let's go back and stay in the old Hidden Den until Carcajou leaves. He would never find us there."

"That is a fine idea, a very good idea," agreed Mrs. Paddletail. And away went the Paddletails across the Wildwood Pond.

Now there was one who had heard about Carcajou who did not worry much. That was Mephitis the Skunk. Mephitis never worried about anything.

When the Laughing Yellow Sun was about to disappear, Mephitis came out of his Friendly Burrow and went for a stroll as usual. Down through the Green Meadow he went, stopping now and then to eat a Fat Grasshopper.

Although Mephitis may have been a sleepy-head and rather slow-witted, still he had sharp ears. There were some people who said his ears were so keen that he could hear where the Plump Grubs were working underground.

From the Green Meadow, Mephitis crossed over the Wide-Wide Pasture to the Woodlot where Virginia Opossum lived, and soon Mephitis was hopping along with his funny gallop right into the Black Forest. Mephitis often went there, for he could find many Plump Grubs around the decaying stumps and logs. It was a fine place to go for a feast.

Mephitis strolled along as if he had not a care in the world. He would stop at an old stump and go rip, rip with his claws, and off would come the bark. Then when the Plump Grubs came tumbling down, he would eat them and go on. Of course if Mephitis could find plenty of Fat Grasshoppers to eat, he would not bother to tear off bark. No, sir; Mephitis did not like to work that well. He did not believe in doing any more work than he had to, and he did not worry, even though Carcajou the Glutton was in the Black Forest right then hunting for someone about his size.

CHAPTER 17

Carcajou the Glutton Gets a Taste

WHEN Carcajou the Glutton reached the Black Forest, one of the first places he went was to Paddletail's Wildwood Pond. And the first thing he did was to climb up on the top of Paddletail's Brushy House and rip a big hole in it.

Carcajou thought he would surely feast on beaver. But, my, how furious he was when he saw that everyone was away!

After that Carcajou went to Danny Muskrat's Grassy House and tore it open. But Danny and Mrs. Muskrat were watching, and down through their underwater doorway they plunged as quick as you could say "scat." Yes, sir; when Carcajou looked in, there was no one in sight.

That did not improve Carcajou's temper one bit. With an awful growl he splashed over to the bank and started around the Wildwood Pond. He was not quite sure where he was going, but it would have been a bad time for anyone to meet him.

As soon as Carcajou left, Danny Muskrat and Mrs. Muskrat came back and repaired their

Grassy House. It was not much trouble for Danny to gather some more Tumbled Bulrushes and Swamp Grass and Green Moss, and fill the hole that Carcajou had made.

When Paddletail saw Danny Muskrat fixing his house, he decided that he would repair his own Brushy House. So he brought Soft Poplar Brush and Bitter Willow Brush and many, many sticks, and laid them crisscross over the hole that Carcajou had torn. Paddletail was careful not to go far from his Wildwood Pond. Yes, sir; he stayed right where he could tumble into the water if danger came near.

In a little while everyone in the Black Forest knew that Carcajou had visited the Wildwood Pond and had torn open Paddletail's and Danny's homes. Tattler the Jay had seen Carcajou when he did it, and soon Tattler was flying through the Black Forest telling everyone he saw. One of the first ones he met was Mephitis the Skunk.

"Beware, beware!" said Tattler the Jay; "Carcajou has torn down Paddletail's Brushy House, and he is terribly angry. Beware, beware!"

But Mephitis did not seem to be worrying about Carcajou. He went right along tending to his business of looking for Fat Grasshoppers. Whatever else Mephitis may have been, he at least believed in letting other people alone if they did not bother him. So he jogged along with his queer gallop, stopping sometimes to look around an old stump or log for Plump Grubs or Tiny the Meadow Mouse.

But Carcajou was one neighbor who did not mind his own business and let other folks alone. He was a troublemaker wherever he went.

Now it happened that as Carcajou started one way around the Wildwood Pond, Mephitis was going the other way around. And there was Carcajou as angry as could be.

Soon Carcajou spied Mephitis digging by an old log. He was making the dirt fly. That was too good a chance for Carcajou to pass by. He

Carcajou ripped a big hole in Paddletail's Brushy House.

thought he would grab Mephitis while he was not looking.

Mephitis was not so sleepyheaded as he looked. Every little while he would raise his head and look around. You see, Mephitis had other enemies besides Carcajou. There were Shaggy the Wolf and Ranger the Coyote and even Great Horn the Owl. Mephitis was watchful even though he did not appear to be.

When Mephitis saw Carcajou coming, he did not even try to run or to hide. No, sir; he stood there with his tail over his back and waited. Mephitis was a big cousin of Spot the Skunk. At least he was larger than Spot. Some called Spot, Mr. Civet; but his real name was Spot the Skunk.

Do you remember about the time when Aquila the Golden Eagle swooped down to catch Johnny Chuck while he was asleep on a rock? And how Spot the Skunk happened to be there and shot Aquila with his queer spray gun? Well, that is what Mephitis did to Carcajou the Glutton when Carcajou came too near. Mephitis had a sprayer just like Spot's, and he shot his sickening odor right into Carcajou's mouth and eyes.

It did not make any difference how angry Carcajou was, or how much he wanted to grab Mephitis, he simply could not stand that odor, and he could scarcely see anything. His eyes burned worse than they would have if they had soap in them.

Down to the Wildwood Pond went Carcajou as fast as he could go. He ran into logs and brush and rocks along the way, because he could not see well. Then he plunged his head right into the water to wash off that strong odor.

"Haw haw haw," laughed someone near by; "now I guess Carcajou will go back to the Big Mountains where he belongs. Haw haw haw."

When Mephitis looked up, there was Tattler the Jay laughing hard enough to split his mouth. Then away Tattler flew to tell everyone he saw about what had happened to Carcajou. That was one time that the little Wild Creatures were glad to listen to what Tattler had to say.

Tattler really should not have been talking about anyone, because he was as bad as Carcajou whenever he had a chance to be. He would rob the nests of his Feathered Friends, and he was always gossiping.

Sometimes we see people who are just like Tattler when it comes to gossiping. They will talk about their neighbors and criticize them, when they do worse things themselves.

CHAPTER 18

Danny Muskrat Visits the Paddletails

"LET'S go over and visit the Paddletails," said Danny Muskrat, after he had finished repairing his Grassy House.

"Yes, I should like to," said Mrs. Muskrat, and away they started across the Wildwood Pond.

You see, the Muskrats and the Paddletails were good friends. Almost every night the Muskrats swam over for a play spell with the Paddletails. First they would visit awhile with the Paddletails in their Brushy House, and then out they would all come together for a game of Water Tag. Perhaps they had a different name for it.

Sometimes Paddletail started the game. He would swim swiftly in a circle and make Silvery Ripples, and then Danny Muskrat would swim through these Silvery Ripples and make some himself. Soon they would all be making Silvery Ripples and having a fine time. At least it looked as if they played the game that way.

When the Muskrats came to Paddletail's Brushy House, down they dove right into Paddletail's Secret Doorway, and soon they came up in-

The Paddletails and the Muskrats
played a game of Water Tag.

side. Now, how do you suppose the Muskrats
knew where Paddletail's Secret Doorway was?
Well, that was a secret between the Muskrats and
the Paddletails.

You see, when Paddletail built his Secret Doorway, he put a nice, white, peeled stick on each side,
which stuck out a way in front. When the Muskrats visited Paddletail, they dived down between
those sticks, and there was the Secret Doorway.
The Muskrats were the only ones who knew anything about Paddletail's Guide Sticks, because
they were the only ones who visited Paddletail in
his home; and they never told anyone about them.

Sometimes Brownie and Silver Paddletail
played in front of their home, and the space be-

(109)

tween the Guide Sticks made a nice front yard for them to play in.

"I see you have your house repaired," said Danny Muskrat; "that was a mean trick that Carcajou the Glutton played on both of us."

"Yes, I have it fixed, and I hope Carcajou does not tear my Brushy House apart again."

"I don't think he will be back right away after what Mephitis the Skunk did to him," said Danny; "but it was what he deserved."

"Oh, let's go out and play," said Silver, and soon the Paddletails and the Muskrats were out in front of the Brushy House having a fine time.

At last the game of Water Tag was over, and it

Paddletail stood up on his hind legs
and braced himself with his tail.

was time for the Muskrats to go back home. They never stayed long when they visited the Paddletails. Perhaps it was because they did not want the Paddletails to grow tired of them.

"Now, what shall we do?" asked Silver Paddletail, after the Muskrats had left.

"Tonight I will teach you how to cut down a tree," said Paddletail.

"Oh, what fun that will be!" said Brownie.

"And then I will cut down a tree all by myself," said Silver.

You see, Brownie and Silver were getting to be quite large, and Paddletail thought it was time for them to learn how to work. He thought they might as well cut down their own trees when they wanted some Tender Buds or Spicy Bark to eat.

"We will go to the Broad Flat, and there I will show you how it is done," he said.

The Young Paddletails were glad to hear that they could go to the Broad Flat again. They jumped around in the water and splashed, and then started to swim toward the Broad Flat.

"Now don't forget to watch for Enemies," said Paddletail. "If I strike the water with my tail, you must dive."

But the Young Paddletails were in a hurry to get to the Broad Flat, and they were not watchful.

Suddenly Paddletail went whack! on the water with his large, flat tail, and dived out of sight. Down went the Young Paddletails also, and they did not come up until they were almost back to the Brushy House again.

"What did you see, father?" asked Brownie.

"I only wanted to see if you were on guard," said Paddletail. Then they all went on to the Broad Flat.

"The first thing to remember is to choose a tree that is not leaning toward another," said Paddletail, "for then it would fall against it and not fall to the ground." So Paddletail found a tree that leaned toward his Secluded Ditch where there was not another tree in the way.

"I wonder if this tree is good," said Paddletail, and he bit off a piece of Spicy Bark to see if he liked it. "Yes, it is all right. First you make a deep cut like this as high up as you can reach."

Paddletail stood up on his hind legs and braced himself with his tail while he made a deep gash in the tree.

"You make this deep cut on the side toward which you want the tree to fall. Then you make another deep cut quite a way below it, and take out the wood between them in a large chip," and Paddletail bit out a large chip to show the Young

Paddletails how it was done. "Then you keep doing that until you have cut more than halfway through before you start to cut on the other side. If the tree is small, sometimes you can cut it down all from one side; but if it is large, you must cut around and around. You must always cut the most from the side where the tree is to fall."

Soon Paddletail's tree went down with a crash, for it was not a large one. Then he helped Brownie and Silver Paddletail to find trees to cut down themselves. Soon they were making the chips fly, and then Paddletail went back to his own fallen tree to eat some Spicy Bark while he watched for Enemies.

CHAPTER 19

Two Thieves Meet

"I BELIEVE I'll go to the Black Forest for a visit," said Chatterer the Red Squirrel one day. "Everything is *so* dull around here."

Chatterer lived in a Hollow Den Tree in the Wide-Wide Pasture near the Green Meadow. The reason why everything seemed so dull to him was that all his neighbors were wise to his tricks and were watching him.

It is not a pleasant thing to say about anyone, but Chatterer was a thief. He had no reason at all to steal from other folks, but he did. There was plenty for everyone to eat. If he was not trying to rob the Secret Storehouses of his cousin Worker the Gray Squirrel, he was trying to steal the eggs from the nest of some Feathered Friend. So everyone had learned to be on guard when Chatterer the Red Squirrel was around.

When Chatterer said that he was going to the Black Forest for a visit, you may be sure that he was planning some mischief. Yes, he thought he would go to the Black Forest and see if he could not find some Round Little Nests to rob. And

Chatterer dropped the pine cone and grabbed an egg.

so away went Chatterer, scolding and chattering at the top of his voice. He surely was a noisy neighbor. He was almost as bad as Noisy the English Sparrow when it came to making a big noise.

"I am glad that Chatterer is going away for a while," said Mrs. Yellow Warbler.

"And so am I," said Mrs. Chat; "perhaps now we can have a little peace."

Worker the Gray Squirrel was glad also, and he started to gather cones and acorns and other goodies and hide them away while Chatterer was not there to watch him. He put them under rocks and in Warm Hollow Logs and in such places where he thought Chatterer would not find them. Sometimes he even dug a little hole in the ground and filled it with cones, though how he ever expected to find them again is a mystery. But Worker had a good memory; and that was one of his secrets.

Chatter, chatter, chatter, and scold, scold, scold, was what Chatterer did everywhere he went, and it wasn't long until everyone in the Black Forest knew that he was there. It was as it is when an undesirable person moves into a neighborhood. Everyone is soon talking about him. But if a good neighbor moves in, they are not so quick to tell about the nice things he does for them.

That is the way it was when Chatterer went to the Black Forest. In a little while everyone was complaining to everyone else about how noisy Chatterer was. And everyone was telling every one else that Chatterer was a mischief-maker. I would not want such a reputation as that, would you?

But Chatterer did not seem to care what anyone thought of him. He did not seem to have any self-respect at all. He went right ahead with his noise and his nest hunting regardless of what anyone said.

One day Chatterer started to climb a Great Pine Tree. He had not had anything to eat that morning, and he was hungry.

Tattler stayed nearer
home after that.

"I believe I'll climb this tree and get a Delicious Pine Cone," said Chatterer.

Up he went, and soon he found one that looked good. Chatterer bit it off and ran back along the limb to the tree trunk to eat it. Then what do you suppose Chatterer saw right there before his very eyes? Why, a Round Little Nest, of course, with some eggs in it. That was too much of a temptation for Chatterer. He dropped that Delicious Pine Cone and grabbed an egg.

Now it happened that that nest belonged to Tattler the Jay, and although Tattler would steal the eggs from other Round Little Nests and so would Mrs. Jay, they did not want anyone to take their eggs. No, sir; that was entirely different.

Mrs. Jay had been out looking for Round Little

Nests herself, and she came home as that Delicious Pine Cone came tumbling down from her tree. Mrs. Jay knew there must be a reason for that, and she thought the reason was Chatterer.

Sure enough, when she flew to a limb near her nest, there sat Chatterer holding one of her eggs between his front feet and eating out of a hole that he had made in one end.

My, how furious that made Mrs. Jay! She called loudly for Tattler to come, and then she flew against Chatterer so hard that she almost knocked him right out of the Great Pine Tree.

Pick, pick, pick, she went with her strong, sharp bill, and you should have seen the way the fur flew out of Chatterer's coat. And then Tattler himself came home to take a hand in it.

Chatterer dropped off the limb on which he was sitting to the one below it, and raced headfirst down that Great Pine Tree. What is more, he did not stop until he was halfway back to his own Hollow Den Tree in the Wide-Wide Pasture. And then how Chatterer did scold!

That should have been a good lesson for the Jays, because they learned what it was like when someone stole their eggs. But the Jays and Chatterer were all born criminals, and it would be hard to change them.

Chatterer was glad to get back to his Hollow Den Tree, and he did not go back to the Black Forest for another visit for a long time. After that the Jays stayed nearer their own home so they could watch their own Round Little Nest instead of bothering their neighbors. So Chatterer the Red Squirrel and the Jays had both done some good for each other even though they did not know it. We can usually see some good in everyone if we will look for it.

CHAPTER 20

Redhead the Woodpecker Brings News

OF all the Feathered Friends on the Old Homestead and in the Black Forest, it is doubtful if there were any that did more traveling than Redhead the Woodpecker. Of course his cousins Judge Flicker and Downy the Woodpecker did much flying around also, but Redhead the Woodpecker did even more than they. He was always on the go.

You see, Redhead the Woodpecker liked to eat many different kinds of things. First he would dine on Tree Borers and other insects, and then he would eat some Tempting Wild Berries for dessert. Then again he might decide to eat some Tiny Little Seeds or pick the inside out of Sweet Acorns.

So Redhead the Woodpecker flew up and down the Wildwood Lanes in the Black Forest and through the Apple Orchard and down to the Woodlot and back to the Big Jungle Thicket from morning until night, looking for something good to eat. If there was anything doing around the Old Homestead, he was sure to see it or hear about it. That was how Redhead happened to discover an interesting bit of news one day.

Redhead had been over to the Apple Orchard to see if he could find some Tree Borers at work on Farmer Smith's apple trees. On his way back to the Black Forest, Redhead thought he would follow along Little River toward Paddletail's Wildwood Pond. There were Tangled Brushes and Twining Vines and Tempting Berries all along Little River to the Black Forest, and Redhead was sure he would have a feast.

Then, as Redhead entered the Black Forest, what do you suppose he saw on the bank of Little River? You never would guess it. It was the Flapping White Tent of Fearful the Man.

"Now what do you suppose Fearful the Man has come here for?" thought Redhead. "I don't believe he is up to any good thing."

But there he was, unpacking boxes and gathering wood and doing many other things that told Redhead he expected to stay awhile. Redhead flew nearer, and perched on the side of a tree to look around. "Tap-tap-tap-tap," he went, for right there in front of his nose was a Tree Borer at work.

"Well, hello there, Redhead," said Fearful the Man. "Did you come over to visit my camp?"

"Tap-tap-tap-tap,"
went Redhead on Paddletail's tree.

That was too much for Redhead, and away he flew as fast as he could to tell some of his neighbors what he had seen.

Not far away he met Trader the Pack Rat outside his Rock Shelter Home.

"I see you have a neighbor," said Redhead.

"And who may that be?" asked Trader the Pack Rat.

"Fearful the Man is living in a Flapping White Tent by Little River around the bend," replied Redhead. Then he flew on toward the Wildwood Pond.

Paddletail was starting his night's work when Redhead lit on the side of the tree that he was cutting.

"Tap-tap-tap-tap," went Redhead on Paddletail's tree. Paddletail looked up to see who was there. He did not know whether it was Judge Flicker or Downy the Woodpecker or Redhead.

"I have some news for you," said Redhead; "Fearful the Man is living in a Flapping White Tent by Little River down by the edge of the Black Forest."

"Now what do you suppose he is doing there?" asked Paddletail.

Redhead did not wait to answer. The Weird Darkness was beginning to cover the Black Forest, and it was time for Redhead to go home to his hole in an Old Hollow Stub by the Big Jungle Thicket.

When Paddletail heard that Fearful the Man

It was the Flapping White
Tent of Fearful the Man.

was living not far away, he was worried. He thought that Fearful had come to the Black Forest to do some kind of mischief, and he told Mrs. Paddletail so. When Danny Muskrat and Mrs. Muskrat came over for a visit, he told them about it. It was not long until all the Woods Folk knew about Fearful the Man and were wondering what he had come to the Black Forest for. They were sure it was for no good.

The Paddletails were the most worried of all. They knew that if Fearful the Man came to the Wildwood Pond, the first thing he would see would be their Brushy House. All the other Furry Friends and Feathered Friends could hide, but there was Paddletail's Home right in plain sight of anyone who cared to look at it.

Danny Muskrat felt the same way about it, but Danny's Grassy House was not in such plain sight. It was smaller, and it was partly hidden by Swamp Grass and Tumbled Bulrushes.

When Tattler the Jay heard that Fearful the Man was living in a Flapping White Tent in the edge of the Black Forest, of course he had to go and see about it. He thought he might find some scraps of food, which Fearful had thrown out, and have a feast.

So Tattler alighted on the limb of a tree not far

from Fearful's Flapping White Tent, and looked around to see what he could find.

"Haw haw haw," he said, "I am glad Pesty the Magpie doesn't know anything about this."

Soon Fearful the Man came out of his Flapping White Tent and went down to Little River after a pailful of Sparkling Water. "Haw haw haw," said Tattler the Jay, and away he flew to a safe distance.

"Well, there is Tattler the Jay already," said Fearful the Man to himself. "It seems as if every place I go Tattler is there to warn the other little Wild Creatures. I wonder if he ever stays at home."

That is what many folks wondered who knew Tattler the Jay. But what Paddletail the Beaver was wondering, and what all the other little Wild Creatures were wondering, was what Fearful the Man was doing there in his Flapping White Tent on the Bank of Little River in the edge of the Black Forest. That was what they wanted to know.

CHAPTER 21

Trader the Pack Rat Investigates

WHEN Redhead the Woodpecker told Trader the Pack Rat that Fearful the Man was living in a Flapping White Tent around a bend of Little River, that was the best news that Trader had heard in a long time.

"I'll go down to Fearful's Flapping White Tent and see if I can find some things I want," said Trader to himself.

So that night when Fearful the Man was sound asleep, Trader left his Rock Shelter Home and slipped along through the Leafy Bushes and Tangled Grass in the direction of Fearful's Flapping White Tent.

"I'll take something along to trade to Fearful the Man," thought Trader.

At last he found a stone that he could carry, and he picked it up in his mouth and took it along with him.

Now it happened that when Fearful the Man had washed his face that night he had left the soap on the log beside his washbasin. That was the first thing Trader saw, and it suited him exactly. Of course Trader had no use for soap, for he never used it when he washed his face. But Trader wanted that soap badly, and so he left the rock that he had brought, and took the soap.

You see, although Trader wanted many things that he did not need at all, he did not believe in stealing. No sir; Trader was covetous, but he was not a thief. He believed in always leaving something in place of what he took.

Did you ever know anyone that collected all kinds of old vases and guns and other things for the fun of it? Of course you have. We call such a man a curio collector. That was what Trader was, a curio collector. He picked up all kinds of queer things for which he had not a bit of use, and piled them around in his Rock Shelter Home.

Trader was willing to exchange something for the thing he wanted, even though he always made a one-sided trade. So after he had left that piece of soap in his Rock Shelter Home, he began to look around for something else to take back with him. At last he decided that a pine cone would do, and back he went to Fearful's Flapping White Tent, carrying a pine cone.

The next thing Trader saw that he wanted was one of Fearful's spoons. It was nice and shiny, and although Trader never ate with a spoon, he dropped the pine cone and took the spoon.

Soon Trader was back again, and this time he brought a chip of wood that he picked up on the way back. Trader certainly was not careful about giving equal value when he made a trade. He was a cheater, for when he saw Fearful's watch on a box by the bed, he traded that old chip of wood for it.

It was a mystery what Trader wanted with a watch, for he never, never needed one; for the Laughing Yellow Sun told him when it was time to go to bed and time to get up, and Trader ate whenever he was hungry. But away he went with Fearful's watch, and soon he was back again, carrying a piece of old bone to trade for something else.

Trader wanted one of Fearful's spoons.

Now it happened that Fearful had left his shoes on the ground by his bed when he had gone to sleep, and Trader the Pack Rat thought one of them would make a nice addition to his collection. Of course Trader never wore shoes, but he wanted one anyway.

Trader laid down the thing he had brought and took hold of the toe of Fearful's shoe. It was much larger than he was, and he could not begin to carry it. All he could do was to drag it along on the ground. That was hard work for Trader, and by the time he had dragged it outside of the tent, he was ready to give it up as a bad job and try something else.

Back into the Flapping White Tent went

Trader took hold of the toe of Fearful's shoe.

Trader the Pack Rat, looking for something that he could carry. It did not take his Black Little Eyes long to see Fearful's comb, and away he went with it as fast as he could go.

I am afraid that if the Laughing Yellow Sun had not come up and put a stop to Trader's work, Fearful the Man would not have had much left. But there it was, peeping out of the east, when Trader arrived at his Rock Shelter Home with the comb; and it was time for Trader to take a nap.

"I'll go back and trade some more after the Laughing Yellow Sun goes down," thought Trader, as he curled up in his Snug Bed.

If you have never seen Trader the Pack Rat, you will know him from his cousin Mr. Barn Rat because he is larger. He is also a different color. Instead of being brown like Mr. Barn Rat, he is a grayish color with almost a cream or white stomach. And Trader's tail is not bare like Mr. Barn Rat's, but has hair on it. Trader's fur is softer and finer than Mr. Barn Rat's, and he has large, round ears.

Sometimes Trader the Pack Rat is called Mr. Wood Rat because he likes to live in the woods. He belongs to the same family as Danny Muskrat, but he is not much like him. Some people like one thing and some like another. Some like to live in the backwoods, while others would rather live near water and be sailors. That is the way it is with Trader the Pack Rat and his cousin Danny Muskrat, for Danny likes water.

Trader is not such a pest as is Mr. Barn Rat, for Trader does not destroy so many things. But he is such a joker that sometimes he is a nuisance. He thinks it is the best kind of joke to carry a large pile of trash into Fearful's Cabin if he can get in, and then to carry away some of Fearful's belongings.

CHAPTER 22

Fearful the Man Misses Some Things

THE same Laughing Yellow Sun that told Trader the Pack Rat that it was time to go to bed told Fearful the Man that it was time to get up. The Bright Little Sunbeams were shining on Fearful's Flapping White Tent when he awoke, and he thought it must be late. But when he reached for his watch, there was no watch in sight.

"Now that is strange," said Fearful the Man; "I am quite sure that I left my watch right there on that box."

Then Fearful looked under his pillow and in his vest pocket, to make certain that he had not forgotten. Of course Fearful did not find his watch, and he wondered where else he might have left it.

"I wonder if my watch dropped out of my pocket when I leaned over to get a pail of water out of Little River," said Fearful.

When Fearful decided to dress and look in Little River for his watch, he could not find one of his shoes. There was one as he had left it; but the other was gone.

"Surely that shoe did not walk away," thought Fearful; "but I can't seem to find it."

When Fearful opened the tent and looked out, there was his shoe lying on the ground with the laces caught in a Stubby Little Bush. There were many Scratchy Little Tracks around it, and Fearful could see where it had been dragged along through the dust.

"I must have had a Furry Visitor last night," said Fearful; "but I hope he did not expect to eat my shoe. I believe I'll take my soap and towel down to Little River and wash up when I go to look for my watch."

But when Fearful looked for his soap, he could not find it.

"I thought surely I left it right here on this log," said Fearful.

Then Fearful noticed something on the log where his soap had been. It was the stone that Trader had left in place of it.

"Aha," said Fearful, "I see that my Furry Visitor was Trader the Pack Rat. He should have known that I cannot use a stone in place of soap."

Then Fearful the Man went in and looked on the box where his watch had been. Sure enough, there was a chip of wood that Trader the Pack Rat had traded for it. And on the ground was the piece of old bone that Trader had left when he started away with the shoe.

"Yes, sir; it was Trader the Pack Rat all right," said Fearful, "and that is where my watch went."

Of course when Fearful wanted to comb his hair, he could not find his comb, and later, when he needed a spoon, he found a pine cone in place of it.

"Now I wonder where Trader lives," said Fearful the Man to himself. "I'll have to see if I can find his home and get my things back."

So after Fearful had eaten his breakfast, he started out through the Wildwood along Little River to see if he could find where Trader lived. Sometimes he could see the Scratchy Little Tracks in the dust, but most of the time he could see nothing.

It happened that while Fearful the Man was out looking for the home of Trader the Pack Rat, he almost ran right into Snowshoe the Hare sitting in a Cozy Form in a Jungle Thicket. You see, sometimes Trader the Pack Rat built a Big Stick Nest in which to live instead of a Rock Shelter Home; and when Fearful saw the Jungle Thicket, he thought Trader might have his home there.

In went Fearful through the Leafy Bushes and Blackberry Brambles, and suddenly almost from

Almost from under
his feet jumped
Snowshoe.

under his feet jumped Snowshoe the Hare. It would be hard to say which one was the more surprised, Fearful the Man or Snowshoe the Hare. Of course Snowshoe thought it was Terror the Hunter, and Fearful thought for a moment that Snowshoe was Forktongue the Snake among the Leafy Bushes.

My, but you may be sure it did not take Snowshoe long to get out of there, and then he went back to his own Willow Thicket on Little River above Paddletail's Wildwood Pond.

After a while Fearful the Man gave up looking in the Jungle Thicket and sat down on a log to think. "Now where do you suppose Trader lives?" was what he was asking himself. "I must find his home and get my watch back. I simply must. I

(135)

wonder if Trader lives among those Tumbled Rock Piles."

So Fearful went to look at the Tumbled Rock Piles to see if he could find the home of Trader. He searched and searched, and was about ready to give up.

"I believe I shall have to go and get Nero the Hound to find Trader's home for me," said Fearful; "it would not take him long to smell it out."

Then, as Fearful was ready to give up, he spied a pile of trash by a Rocky Ledge, and it did not take him long to see that he had found Trader's Rock Shelter Home. Dig, dig, dig, went Fearful in the trash pile, but his watch was not there. Then he cut a long pole with a hook on the end of it, and he began to drag out more trash from Trader's Rock Shelter Home. You see, Fearful could not get at Trader's home any other way because the Tumbled Rock Piles would not let him.

With almost the first bunch of trash that Fearful dragged out, he found his comb and spoon. And then right away he saw his watch back in between two large rocks.

"I am sorry to have to tear Trader's home to pieces," said Fearful, as he dragged out another bunch of trash with his pole; "but I must have my watch. And, besides, he hasn't anything else to do but fix his home again. Perhaps that will keep him out of mischief for a while."

Fearful was certainly glad to find his watch in good condition and still keeping time.

When Trader the Pack Rat awakened from his Snug Bed to go trading again, what a surprise he had to find all his new loot gone!

You may be sure that after that Fearful the Man kept his belongings in boxes where Trader could not get at them.

CHAPTER 23

A Break in Paddletail's Dam

"WELL, I am ready to visit Paddletail the Beaver," said Fearful the Man the next morning after he had got his watch back from Trader the Pack Rat. "Yes, I believe I will go to Paddletail's Wildwood Pond this morning."

Fearful the Man tied the front of his Flapping White Tent together and started toward Paddletail's High Dam. There were many Jungle Thickets along Little River, so Fearful did not follow closely along the Brushy Banks. He did not like to walk through the Leafy Bushes and Blackberry Brambles and Twining Vines.

At last Fearful peeped through the trees ahead of him, and right before his eyes was Paddletail's Wildwood Pond. "My, what a beautiful Wildwood Pond Paddletail has!" exclaimed Fearful. "And right there is his Brushy House in plain sight. I do believe that I see the top of Danny Muskrat's Grassy House sticking up above the Swamp Grass."

Fearful the Man made his way slowly to Paddletail's High Dam, being careful not to leave any signs that would frighten Paddletail away. Out to the middle of it he went, right past the home of Ouzel the Dipper, without seeing it. Then what do you suppose Fearful the Man did? Well, sir, he took a big stick and made a large hole in Paddletail's High Dam.

Fearful knew that when Paddletail found out there was a hole in his High Dam he would come there to repair it. Fearful the Man wanted Paddletail to come out and expose himself.

Of course Paddletail the Beaver did not know that Fearful had torn a large hole in his High Dam. Paddletail was sound asleep in his Brushy House. He had been working all night, and had just gone to sleep. Fearful the Man knew that Paddletail was asleep and would not get up until evening. So Fearful had gone back to his Flapping White Tent after he had made a large hole in Paddletail's High Dam. He thought he would rest until it was time for Paddletail to get up.

The Black Forest was covered with Weird Darkness when Paddletail decided it was time to get up and go to work. The first thing Paddletail did was to dive into his Secret Doorway, expecting to swim outside. But, instead, he went kerplunk into the Oozy Mud, for there was no water in it.

"Oh, dear, the High Dam must have broken,"

said Paddletail. "That will never do, for a Furry Enemy might come along and walk right into this Brushy House. I must go and repair it at once."

You see, when Fearful made a large hole in Paddletail's High Dam, the water ran out through it. Soon the Wildwood Pond began to grow smaller and smaller, and in a little while there was Paddletail's Brushy House without any water around it. That is why Paddletail knew that something had happened to his High Dam.

About the same time that Paddletail decided he would get up and go to work, Mrs. Muskrat awoke also.

"Danny, Danny, wake up!" she cried; "something has happened to Paddletail's High Dam, and there is no water around our Grassy House. I am afraid that Trailer the Mink will come along and see our Secret Doorway, for it is not hidden at all."

You may be sure that it did not take the Muskrats long to go outside. When there was no water around their Grassy House, it was the same as leaving the door open, for then anyone could walk right in.

When Paddletail saw the large hole in his High Dam, he did not waste any time getting to work. No, sir. He examined that hole first from one side of his High Dam and then from the other, to see what would be needed to fix it. Then away he went through the water as fast as he could swim. You see, Fearful the Man had not made the hole large enough to run all the water out of the Wildwood Pond. He emptied out only enough so that Paddletail would know something was wrong.

Of course Paddletail could not use his Secluded Ditches, because there was now no water in them. But he was wise, and he had stored a pile of material handy so he would have it to use if the High Dam ever broke.

Soon Paddletail came back with a long willow stick, which he pushed down into the High Dam at the large hole. After that he brought another and another and stuck them along in a row beside

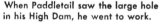

When Paddletail saw the large hole
in his High Dam, he went to work.

the first one. Then he found a large pole and put it across to bind all of them together.

"I don't like the way those sticks stick up above the High Dam," said Paddletail.

So he started in at one side and cut all of them off even with his cross pole. By that time Paddletail was very hungry, and he ate the Spicy Bark from some of the sticks he had cut off. Then he began to carry loads of clay and trash with which to close the openings between the brush framework he had made.

Suddenly there was a blinding flash. It seemed almost as if the Smiling Moon had exploded. Paddletail thought that surely Terror the Hunter had fired at him with his Flashing Gun, so Paddletail whacked a loud warning on the water with his broad tail and dived out of sight.

"Ha ha!" laughed Fearful the Man; "that will be a dandy picture of Paddletail."

You see, Fearful the Man had come to the Wildwood Pond to get a picture of Paddletail. So he had set up his camera near the large hole he had made in the High Dam, and he had set off a large flashlight right when Paddletail was at work repairing his dam. That was why Fearful had been living in a Flapping White Tent on the bank of Little River in the edge of the Black Forest.

CHAPTER 24

Prophet the Cuckoo Predicts Rain

"COWK-COWK-COWK-COWK," shouted Prophet the Cuckoo, which was his way of saying: "We shall have rain soon."

Paddletail the Beaver was back at work again repairing his High Dam after Fearful the Man had torn a large hole in it. Paddletail did not have it quite finished when Fearful set off his flashlight and frightened him away. Then Paddletail was afraid to go back to work that night. He preferred to wait until morning.

"I must hurry and finish this High Dam," said Paddletail. "Prophet the Cuckoo says that rain is coming soon, and the High Dam must be made strong again so it will not wash away if a Foaming Flood comes down."

So Paddletail and Mrs. Paddletail and Brownie and Silver all worked together to finish repairing the High Dam.

"Cowk-cowk-cowk-cowk," said Prophet the Cuckoo again; "get ready for rain in a day or two."

So all the little Wild Creatures began to hurry around and prepare for rainy weather.

"I must fix my Cozy Form," said Snowshoe the Hare to Drummer the Grouse. "Prophet the Cuckoo says it is going to rain soon." Then Snowshoe ran and put new sides on his Cozy Form, after which he ate his fill of Tender Green Things so he would not have to venture out when everything was covered with Wet Little Raindrops.

"I must get something to eat before it rains," said Trader the Pack Rat; "it is so disagreeable running around in wet weather."

Even Farmer Smith heard Prophet the Cuckoo predict rain, and he hurried to get his hay stacked before it got wet.

Of course there were some of the Furry Friends and Feathered Friends who did not mind rain. In fact, they liked it. You would never hear Danny Muskrat complaining about wet weather, for he liked the feel of the Wet Little Raindrops on his back while he was swimming. And the Mallards, who lived on the Duck Pond, quacked for joy whenever it rained. Killdeer the Plover and Jack Snipe and Sicklebill the Curlew and Longbill the Rail and Diver the Grebe and many others at the Duck Pond were also glad to hear that it was going to rain. What a noise Croaker the Frog made!

Then there was Miner the Mole. Of course he was always glad to see a rain, for it made the earth

"Cowk-cowk-cowk-cowk, "said Prophet.
"Get ready for rain."

softer for him to dig in, and it also brought the
Wriggly Earthworms to the top of the ground
where he could get them. And Robin Red always
had a feast after every rain.

"Cowk-cowk-cowk-cowk," said Prophet the
Cuckoo; "get ready for rain."

Now it was a mystery how Prophet the Cuckoo
could tell so long ahead that it was going to rain.
But he did, and no mistake. Sometimes it would
be two or three days before it rained, but Prophet
seldom missed. He was so good at predicting rain
that some people called him Rain Crow, although
he was not a crow at all, and did not look like one.
Perhaps they thought his "cowk-cowk-cowk-
cowk" sounded like a crow.

Prophet the Cuckoo was a sort of bluish slate color, with white on his stomach and tail bottom. He was somewhat the color of Scrapper the King-bird, but not quite so dark, and his body was slim. Prophet had a rather fan-shaped tail when it was spread, and altogether he was almost twice as long as Scrapper the Kingbird. No, sir; Prophet certainly did not look at all like Jim Crow.

Prophet the Cuckoo had the strangest cousin you ever saw. His name was Mr. Road Runner, but some people called him Chaparral Cock. There were none of Prophet's cousins on the Old Homestead, because, you see, they live in the Dusty Southwest.

Mr. Road Runner ate the queerest things imaginable. He ate almost any living thing he could

Mr. Road Runner was Prophet's cousin.

swallow. He was especially fond of lizards and snakes and centipedes, and sometimes he caught mice and insects.

One of the strange things about Mr. Road Runner was that he would seldom fly. Whenever he was frightened, instead of flying he would run along a path or road as fast as his long, strong legs would carry him.

If you were to see Mr. Road Runner, you would never dream that he was Prophet the Cuckoo's cousin, for he did not look anything like him. Mr. Road Runner had quite a topknot on his head, and he was almost as large as a small crow, with a long tail and quite a large beak.

Sometimes the Little Mexican Boys where he lived liked to run a foot race with Mr. Road Runner, and if you had been where he lived, perhaps you would have liked to see if you could outrun him. At least you would have had a hard time to make him fly.

But here we are talking about Mr. Road Runner and forgetting all about Prophet the Cuckoo. You see, Prophet was timid, and if it were not for his "cowk-cowk-cowk-cowk," you would scarcely know there was such a bird around. He liked to hide in the Black Forest where no one would be likely to see him.

Did you ever hear grandpa say that he could tell every time it was going to rain, because his rheumatism hurt him? Perhaps that is how Prophet the Cuckoo knows when a rain is coming; he often knows it before there is a sign of rain. But then, that is his secret. Did you ever hear of a bird's having rheumatism?

Chapter 25

Screecher the Owl Has His Fun

"HO-HUM," said Screecher the Owl, as he awoke from an all-day snooze. "I am hungry, and there is Prophet the Cuckoo saying that it is going to rain. Oh, well, I'll fly over to the Old Homestead and get something to eat and come back home before the rain starts. It really is an ideal night for hunting. Ho-hum."

Away flew Screecher into the Long Shadows. You see, as Prophet the Cuckoo had said, a rain was coming. The sky was covered with Gray Cloud Ships that hid the Smiling Moon's face, and it was sure to be a dark night. But Screecher liked dark nights. His eyes were made to see better at night than during the day. So he was more successful when he hunted on dark nights.

Screecher lived in a hole in an Old Hollow Stub in the Black Forest near the Big Jungle Thicket. Although he was not an especially good neighbor to the other little Wild Creatures, still he was not so bad as he might have been. He was not nearly so bad a neighbor as was his big cousin Great Horn the Owl. But, then, Screecher was only a third as large as Great Horn, so he could not have pounced upon some of the larger creatures if he had wanted to.

Why, Great Horn would even kill Snoop the Weasel and Mephitis the Skunk if he had a chance. And he was more than a match for Hooknose the Chicken Hawk. Yes sir; almost everyone feared Great Horn the Owl, and especially did Snowshoe the Hare, and Jimmy the Swamp Rabbit, and Peter and Molly Cottontail fear him.

Screecher was fond of Fat Grasshoppers and other insects. He also liked mice. That was why he liked to hunt in the Green Meadow and the Wide-Wide Pasture. You see, in the Black Forest, where Screecher lived, there were not many Fat

The Mallards quacked for joy whenever it rained.

"Ho-Hum," said Screecher the Owl.

Grasshoppers, because Mr. Grasshopper preferred to live in the Hot Sunshine. He did not care for the Cool Shade of the Black Forest.

Sometimes Screecher liked to hunt around the Duck Pond. He liked to hunt for Pinchtoes the Crawfish and Croaker the Frog. Usually he hunted along Little River on his way from the Black Forest to the Old Homestead, because sometimes Pinchtoes and Croaker were there. So when Screecher left his home in the Old Hollow Stub, away he flew toward Little River.

Now there was one thing about Screecher that was not at all nice, and that was that he would murder his own brother or sister if he were real hungry. Of course they would have killed Screecher as quickly as he would have killed them, so it was an even fight. We read in the Bible that

Cain became angry at his brother Abel and slew him. Screecher was a Cain in the bird world.

It happened that about the time that Screecher left his home in the Old Hollow Stub and started toward the Old Homestead, Bud Smith was ready to carry in the wood for the night. You see, Bud usually filled the Woodbox before dark, but when the Gray Cloud Ships began to sail across the sky and Prophet the Cuckoo said rain was coming, Bud had to help his mother put Old Cluck and her Chicklets to bed for the night. It would never do to leave them out in the Wet Little Raindrops, and, besides, Snoop the Weasel or Great Horn the Owl might come along and take some of them. They had to be put under shelter.

So by the time Old Cluck and her Chicklets were put safely in their Little Red Coop, it was quite dark outside.

"This is certainly going to be a dark night," said Bud; "look at those Gray Cloud Ships sailing across the sky."

"Yes, and Prophet the Cuckoo has been warning us all day that a rain is coming," said Bud's mother. "How glad the Thirsty Little Flowers will be for a good shower!"

"Listen to those Mallards on the Duck Pond," said Bud; "they must know it is going to rain."

"You must hurry now and carry in the wood before it gets darker," said Mrs. Smith; "it looks as if it would start to rain any minute."

Out to the Woodshed went Bud in the Weird Darkness. He could scarcely see the pile of wood, but he had been there so often he knew right where to find it. Soon he was returning with a large armful, which he stacked evenly in the Hungry Woodbox back of the Shining Kitchen Stove. Back he went after more, until the Hungry Woodbox was almost full.

"I believe I will get one more armful for good measure," said Bud; "then we shall be all set for a rainy night." And he hurried for the last armful that the Hungry Woodbox would hold.

"My, but it surely is dark tonight!" he said to himself, as he came out of the Woodshed and started back toward the Grand Old House. "It is the kind of night that Sneak the Cougar likes to go hunting."

Suddenly there was a terrific scream that seemed to come from the Apple Orchard near by. It sounded something like "Hoe-hoe-hoe-hoe-ee-ah!" and it was terribly shrill and chattering. Bud was so surprised that he dropped his armful of wood and ran toward the Grand Old House as fast as he could.

"My, what is the matter?" asked Bud's mother. "You look as if you had seen a ghost."

Of course Mrs. Smith knew there are no such things as ghosts, but that was her way of saying that Bud looked frightened.

"Didn't you hear that terrible noise?" asked Bud.

"Oh, that was only Screecher the Owl," laughed Mrs. Smith.

Then Bud went back after the wood he had dropped, feeling rather sheepish.

"You can't frighten me again, Mr. Screecher," he said.

CHAPTER 26

A Visitor From the Air

IT was a beautiful day in the fall when the little Wild Creatures on the Old Homestead and in the Black Forest were given their greatest fright. You see, fall on the Old Homestead was a beautiful time of year. It was also a busy time for many of the little Wild Creatures.

When Jack Frost sneaked down from the Land of Cold Breezes and began to paint the Dancing Little Leaflets with gold and red and yellow and brown, the little Wild Creatures knew that it would not be long until Old Man Winter would come along and drop a Soft White Blanket over everything.

So those who stayed on the Old Homestead all year round had much work to do getting ready for the Cold-Cold Days. Of course the Feathered Friends who left for the Sunny Southland every fall did not have anything to do until they arrived in the Land of Sunshine. Then they went to work and made new homes if they wanted them.

But, my, you should have seen how busy some of the little Wild Creatures were! There was

Worker the Gray Squirrel, who had to gather nuts and acorns and grain and cones to fill his Secret Storehouses. And there was his worthless cousin Chatterer the Red Squirrel, who would steal from Worker's Secret Storehouses if he could find them.

There were some of the little Wild Creatures who did not worry about the coming of Old Man Winter. One of these was Johnny Chuck. All he did was to eat and grow fat, or lie stretched out on a flat rock by his Friendly Burrow and sleep in the Warm Sunshine and let the Bright Little Sunbeams dance through the hair on his broad back.

Another one that did not mind Old Man Winter was Redhead the Woodpecker. You see, Red-

Johnny Chuck did not worry about
the coming of Old Man Winter.

head did not need to make a new home, for he had the Old Hollow Stub to live in if he wanted it. And he did not need to gather a supply of food as Worker the Gray Squirrel did, for he could pick out Tree Borers all winter long when he wanted them. All he had to do was to fly through the Black Forest or the Apple Orchard and look for them. Sometimes, if the weather was too cold, Redhead would go to the Sunny Southland; but he never could quite make up his mind whether to go or not until the last minute.

Dandy the Chickadee and Judge Flicker and Pesty the Magpie and Tattler the Jay never worried either. Sometimes it was rather hard for Dandy and Judge Flicker to find enough to eat.

Snoop the Weasel was out, as usual, looking for someone to pounce on.

But Pesty the Magpie usually knew where there was a carcass on which he could dine, and it was a stormy day indeed when Pesty's criminal cousin Tattler the Jay could not find enough dried berries and other things to eat. Sometimes, if Tattler was real hungry, he would visit the Old Homestead and steal Old Cluck's food or anything else he could find.

Of course Sneak the Cougar did not mind seeing the Great Wide World covered with a Soft White Blanket, for then it was harder for Lightfoot the Deer to run away from him. And Shadow the Lynx rather liked it because he could then follow the trail of Snowshoe the Hare.

So there were many of the little Wild Creatures that did not have to make their Snug Beds or fill Secret Storehouses before Old Man Winter arrived. But those that did were always busy during the hazy fall days.

Mephitis the Skunk had not quite decided where he would make his Snug Bed, so he was looking for a Hidden Burrow that suited him.

Shaggy the Wolf and Ranger the Coyote were both teaching their Furry Little Pups how to hunt so they could catch their own food. Snoop the Weasel and Trailer the Mink were out, as usual, looking for someone to pounce on. And one by

It was only Scooter the Airplane.

one the Feathered Friends were leaving for the Sunny Southland.

One of the first to leave the Old Homestead was Spink the Bobolink and his large family. You see, Spink always went early so he could stop in the Rice Fields and get fat before going on to his winter home.

The Bluebirds, who lived in a Nesting Box near the Grand Old House, were never in a hurry to go south. They had left the Old Homestead for a while, but they were only visiting in the Big Mountains. Sometimes they did not start for the Sunny Southland until after the Merry Little Snowflakes had fallen; but they were never in too big a hurry to come back to the Old Homestead for a visit and to see the Nesting Box before they left.

Even Farmer Smith was busier than usual, harvesting his crops and hauling wood and cutting the Rustling Corn and making it into Rustling Corn Shocks.

Yes, sir; it was a busy day when the little Wild Creatures were given the scare of their lives.

All at once, while everyone was at work, there came out of the sky a roaring birdlike thing that was many, many times larger than Baldy the Eagle. It sailed over the Black Forest and above the Old Homestead like a great bird looking for something to swoop down upon. My, how the little Wild Creatures hurried for their Friendly Burrows and for Hiding Places! Even Old Sorrel and Old Bent Horn ran frantically around the Wide-Wide Pasture.

Of course it was only Scooter the Airplane, but it surely did frighten the little Wild Creatures, for it was the first one they had ever seen. They did not know what to make of it.

"Oh, there goes Scooter the Airplane," said Mary. "Isn't it a beauty?"

"I should say it is," said Bud. "Some day I am going to fly an airplane myself, and then I can see what the Old Homestead looks like from high up in the air.

Chapter 27

Brownie and Silver Are Promised an Excursion

"HOW would you like to go on a trip?" asked Paddletail the Beaver one day.

"Oh, wouldn't that be fun?" said Brownie Paddletail.

"I should say it would be," said Silver.

"It is about time we went on a vacation," said Mrs. Paddletail; "I have not had a rest all summer."

"Very well," said Paddletail, "we will go on a trip."

"Where are we going?" asked Brownie Paddletail.

"And when shall we start?" asked Silver.

"We will start tomorrow night," replied Paddletail, "and we will go until we find a new home."

"Shall we leave our Brushy House never to return?" asked Brownie.

"And shall we never see Danny Muskrat again?" asked Silver.

"Perhaps we will come back to our Wildwood

"My, but I am hungry!" said Fisher the Bold.

Pond some day, and if we do we shall see Danny," said Paddletail.

Now it may seem like a strange thing to do to move away and leave a perfectly good home, but that is usually what most Beavers do. You see, they are somewhat like a family of children who go away to college after they grow up. But there was no Beaver college where Paddletail could send his grown-up children, and so he had to go with them to teach them as they went along.

There were many things that the Young Beavers must learn so that some day they could build a High Dam of their own, and know where to build it so the Foaming Floods would not wash it away, and how to repair it if by chance it was damaged. They would have to learn more about the Great Wide World, and how to travel without getting lost, and where to build their Brushy House, and how to store food for winter.

Yes, there were many, many things that Brownie and Silver Paddletail must learn before they could really take care of themselves; and Paddletail thought the best way to teach them was to take them on a trip.

So one night when Danny Muskrat and Mrs. Muskrat were ready to go back to their Grassy House after they had had their usual visit with the Paddletails, the Paddletails told them they were going away.

"But you must be careful," said Danny. "Snowshoe the Hare told me that Fisher the Bold was out hunting in the Black Forest, and he may catch you."

"We will watch out for him," said Paddletail.

Then the Paddletails told Danny and Mrs. Muskrat good-by and started on their long trip up Little River.

"You must stay close to me, or a Furry Enemy will get you," said Paddletail. "You will not have a Brushy House to run into if Shaggy the Wolf or Fisher the Bold or Sneak the Cougar comes along. You must stay close by me, I say."

"Yes, we must watch for Fisher the Bold," said Mrs. Paddletail.

There were many new things for Brownie and Silver to see. As the Paddletails were not very fast travelers, they did not go far the first night. When the Golden Streamers began to shoot up in the east and chase the Weird Darkness away, it was time for the Paddletails to look for a place to sleep.

Have you ever been traveling and wondered where you would sleep when night came? No doubt that is how Brownie and Silver Paddletail felt. But Paddletail had traveled before, and he was wise. It did not take him long to find a pile of Jumbled Logs where a tree that had tried to grow too close to Little River had caved over and broken down some others when it fell.

"This is the place we need," said Paddletail. "We can pile some of these Brushy Limbs on top to hide us."

Soon the Paddletails were sound asleep under that pile of Jumbled Logs, and not far away Fisher the Bold had crawled into a Large Brush Pile and gone to sleep also. Of course the Paddletails did not know that Fisher the Bold was so near. And Fisher the Bold did not know that the Paddletails were sleeping not far away. He thought they were still in their Brushy House at the Wildwood Pond.

That night, at about the time when Danny Muskrat would have been coming over to see them if they had been in their Brushy House, the Paddletails came out of the pile of Jumbled Logs.

"We must have something to eat before we go on," said Paddletail.

"Yes, we must eat some Spicy Bark," said Mrs. Paddletail.

It did not take Paddletail long to find a Little Aspen Tree that suited his taste, and with the help of the others it was soon cut down. Then how they did eat the Tender Buds and Spicy Bark.

Now it happened that while the Paddletails were cutting down their tree, Fisher the Bold came out of his Large Brush Pile and looked around.

Paddletail found a Little Aspen Tree that suited his taste.

"My, but I am hungry!" he said. "I wonder what I can find to eat." And then he went down to Little River to see if he could catch a fish.

When Fisher the Bold was almost to Little River, he heard a noise. It was the sound of a tree falling. Crash! it went. It was far away, but not too far away for Fisher the Bold to be mistaken.

"Now who do you suppose cut down that tree?" Fisher the Bold asked himself. "I did not know there were any Beavers near here. I wonder if Paddletail is taking his family on an outing. I believe I shall slip over that way and find out. My, wouldn't young beaver taste good!" And away went Fisher the Bold toward the place where he had heard the tree fall.

Fisher knew that he would never dare to pounce upon one of the Young Beavers while Paddletail and Mrs. Paddletail were with them. That would never do. Paddletail had long, chisellike teeth, and, what is more, he knew how to use them. But Fisher the Bold thought he might find Brownie or Silver alone, and then he would not be afraid.

CHAPTER 28

Silver Paddletail Meets Fisher the Bold

"WE must be going," said Paddletail the Beaver, after they had eaten their breakfast. You see, the Paddletails had a long way to go, and they were in a hurry. So when Fisher the Bold found the Little Aspen Tree where the Paddletails had eaten breakfast, they were gone.

Now Fisher the Bold was not easily discouraged. No, he did not give up that easily. "I will follow the Paddletails, and perhaps I shall get a chance to pounce on one of them," he said. So he followed up Little River after the Paddletails.

Fisher the Bold belonged to the family of murderers of which we have read before. It was quite a large family, and some were worse than others. But Fisher the Bold was one of the worst. He could even catch and kill his cousin Killer the Marten, and that was quite a feat, for Killer could run around through the tree tops as well as did Chatterer the Red Squirrel.

When it came to tree climbing, Fisher the Bold was better than any of them. He could run up and down trees almost as if he were flying, and when he was in a hurry he jumped across from one tree to another and dropped from one limb to another.

Fisher the Bold could certainly climb trees, and he was also swift on the ground. He was so active that he could catch and kill Furry Friends that were much larger than himself, and that was why he was so greatly feared.

"We must all stay together," said Paddletail the Beaver, as they walked along. "We might meet Fisher the Bold."

"Yes, we will all stay together," said Mrs. Paddletail.

But soon Silver Paddletail got behind. First there was Paddletail in the lead, and next was Mrs. Paddletail, and then Brownie Paddletail, and last came Silver. That is the way they were walking along.

At last Silver became hungry. She stopped to eat some Spicy Bark from a Quaking Aspen Tree, and the first thing she knew the others had gone on without her, and she was alone.

"Oh, dear, I must hurry and catch up," she said, but she stopped to take one more bite of Spicy Bark. Of course Silver would not have stopped if she had known that right then Fisher the Bold's Black Little Eyes were peeping at her across a

Fisher could even catch his cousin, Killer the Marten.

bend in Little River. No, she would not have waited to take another bite of Spicy Bark if she had known that.

"Well, well," said Fisher the Bold to himself; "if there isn't Silver Paddletail eating some Spicy Bark. Now I wonder if she is all alone."

So Fisher the Bold slipped around through Leafy Bushes and over Jumbled Logs toward the place where he had seen Silver. He thought he would get right close, and then he could pounce upon her before she saw him.

But Fisher the Bold had not been quite careful enough. Once when he hopped up and ran along on a log for a way Silver happened to be looking.

"Oh, dear; there is Fisher the Bold!" she said. "Now what shall I do?"

Away she ran as fast as she could on her short

legs. But Silver was fat, and she could not run fast.

"Aha," said Fisher the Bold, when he came to the Quaking Aspen Tree where Silver had been eating and found that she had left, "Silver must have seen me, and left. Well, I'll hurry along and catch her, for I do believe she is alone."

Of course it would not take Fisher the Bold long to catch up with Silver, for he could jump right over Jumbled Logs and slip through the Tangled Brush. Silver was too fat to do that. She knew that Fisher the Bold would soon catch her.

My, how she wished that she had not stopped to eat Spicy Bark or that she was back at the Wildwood Pond where she could dive out of sight! But Little River was too small for much swimming. That was why Paddletail had built his High Dam.

As Silver was wondering what to do, she came to a Broad Bend. There was a Quiet Pool, with a Large Tumbled-Down Tree in the water, and between the Large Tumble-Down Tree and the bank there was a Long Tunnel. Silver backed into the Long Tunnel, and hid.

When Fisher the Bold came along, he rushed right past Silver's Hiding Place before he knew it, and there was no Silver in sight.

"Now, where do you suppose Silver Paddletail went so quickly?" said Fisher the Bold to himself.

"I am sure that she cannot be far away. I believe I will look and see if she is hiding near here."

"Sniff, sniff," went Fisher the Bold along the bank of Little River. "Here are the tracks of Paddletail," said Fisher the Bold. "Sniff, sniff; and here are Mrs. Paddletail's tracks. Sniff, sniff; and these are Brownie Paddletail's." But although Fisher the Bold sniffed here and there, he could not find Silver's tracks.

Then he went back where he had last seen Silver, and sniffed. Sure enough, the Playful Air Whiffs told him as plainly as anything that Silver had been along there.

"Sniff, sniff," went Fisher the Bold as he walked along, and in a little while the Playful Air Whiffs had led him straight to the Large Tumbled-Down Tree. "Well, well, I see a Long Tunnel by that tree. Now, I wonder if Silver Paddletail could be hiding in there."

Down to the Long Tunnel jumped Fisher the Bold, and looked in. And right there, with her chisellike teeth showing, sat Silver Paddletail, looking out.

CHAPTER 29

The Paddletails Meet Old Friends

WHEN Fisher the Bold saw Silver glaring at him, he hardly knew what to do. You see, he had expected to surprise her and pounce upon her when she was not looking. But there she was in a Long Tunnel where he could not spring on her; the only way he could get to her was to face those chisellike teeth.

So Fisher the Bold explored along the Large Tumbled-Down Tree to see if he could find another doorway to the Long Tunnel. He thought he might get into it and catch Silver from behind. But there was no other doorway into it, so back to the open end went Fisher the Bold.

Slowly he crawled toward Silver, looking for a chance to spring when she was not watching him closely. But Silver sat there and waited with her mouth open; and there they were glaring at each other when down dropped Paddletail off the bank right on Fisher's back.

Over into the Quiet Pool they rolled, and then down out of sight they sank. Of course Paddletail was right at home in the water, and soon the Quiet

Pool was clouded with mud, which they stirred up as they went round and round.

At last Fisher the Bold tore loose from Paddletail's strong teeth, and you may be sure that he did not waste any time getting away from there. No, sir; that was the last that the Paddletails saw of Fisher the Bold.

When the Paddletails started on their journey again, Silver was more careful to stay with the others. I should say she was! And she watched out for Furry Enemies, too. That was how she happened to be the first to see some Shadowy Forms coming down Little River one evening after they had started out on their night's hike. The Shadowy Forms were too far away for her to

Fisher the Bold hardly knew what to do.

see what they were; but she was sure she had seen something.

"Oh, I saw some Shadowy Forms!" said she; "I wonder what they can be."

"I hope they are not Furry Enemies," said Brownie.

Then the Paddletails stopped and watched. Sure enough, there were Shadowy Forms, six of them. So the Paddletails waited. Nearer and nearer they came, until they were straight across Little River from the Paddletails. Who do you suppose they were?

Well, sir, they were some old neighbors of the Paddletails, and their name was Flattail. You see, once upon a time Paddletail and his family and Flattail the Beaver and his family had lived side by side in a Big Colony House. So they were very good friends.

Do you know what a Big Colony House is? It is something like an apartment house. You see, it is like this: First a family of Beavers like the Paddletails build a Brushy House, as Paddletail had done at the Wildwood Pond. Then when it is finished, along come another family of Beavers like the Flattails, and they build another Brushy House right beside the first one. Sometimes a third family will come along and build a third house right against the other two. After that all the Beavers work together and put a large roof over all three Brushy Houses so that it looks like one Big Brushy House.

When two or three families of people live in one house, we say it is an apartment house; but when two or three families of Beavers live like that, we call it a Big Colony House.

Once upon a time the Paddletails and the Flattails had lived together in a Big Colony House, but each family had had its own home. The Paddletails and the Flattails were indeed glad to see one another. Brownie and Silver had never seen any of the Flattails, and the four Young Flattails had never seen any of the Paddletails. But it did not take them long to get acquainted.

"Well, well, where are you going?" asked Paddletail.

"We are looking for a new home," answered Flattail. "And where are you going?"

"We are looking for a new home also," said Paddletail.

The Flattails were taking their children on a trip as the Paddletails were doing.

"Suppose we trade Brushy Houses for a while," said Flattail. "We have a fine large one up Little River a way, and there is a High Dam and a Wildwood Pond and everything. But we wanted a change."

"That is a fine idea," said Paddletail. "You will find our Brushy House and High Dam and Wildwood Pond about three nights' journey down Little River. And will you please tell Danny Muskrat 'hello' for us?"

So, as the custom was among beavers, the Paddletail family and the Flattail family agreed to trade homes.

"I am sure that you will like our old home," said Paddletail. "It is in the Black Forest on the Old Homestead, and we have many, many friends there. Danny Muskrat is a good neighbor, and he will come over to visit you almost every night."

"Oh, let's go on to our new home," said one of the Flattails.

"Yes, I think we shall like it as well as our old one," said another.

Away went the Flattails down Little River toward Paddletail's Wildwood Pond in the Black Forest, while the Paddletails went up Little River in search of the home they got in exchange for it.

"I wonder if we will like our new home," said Mrs. Paddletail, as they walked along. "You know, somehow I didn't want to leave our own home in the Black Forest. I would rather have stayed right there. But I suppose it will be more interesting for the children in a new home, and, besides, they needed to see some of the Great Wide World."

"I suppose they did," said Paddletail; "but I liked our old home myself."

As they hurried on they thought about all the happy times they had enjoyed in the Wildwood Pond on the Old Homestead. They almost wished they were back in their Grassy House. It had been such fun to build it even though it had required a lot of work.

CHAPTER 30

The Paddletails' New Home

DID you ever hear that soon you were to move into a new home? Do you remember how anxious you were to see it? Well, that is the way that Brownie and Silver Paddletail felt when they heard about their new home. They could hardly wait to see it.

"Oh, let's hurry, let's hurry!" was all they seemed to be able to say.

Of course it really was time for them to find a home somewhere, for the nights were growing colder and colder. Every night Jack Frost stole out with his paintbrush and tried to see how beautiful he could make the Dancing Little Leaflets.

First he painted the Quaking Aspens yellow. Then he colored the Maples and Ivy a bright red. After that he seemed to have some brown and gold paint left, and he went about dabbing paint right and left until everything but the Evergreens was colored. Of course it would never do to paint all the trees, so he left some of them green.

Yes, sir; the nights certainly were getting cold, and that made the Paddletails anxious to find a

When two or three families of Beavers live in one home, we call it a Big Colony House.

home; for Paddletail the Beaver had much work to do before Old Man Winter arrived. When you see Jack Frost painting everything, you may be sure that Old Man Winter is not far away.

So the Paddletails hurried onward toward their new home, for they had to gather much Soft Poplar Wood for food before the Wildwood Ponds froze over; because after that they would not be able to get any, you see.

If you want to know how Paddletail stored his Soft Poplar Wood so he could get to it after his Wildwood Pond was frozen, and what Danny Muskrat did, and how the other Furry Friends and Feathered Friends lived during cold weather, you will want to read the book entitled *Wild Creatures in Winter,* for that is another story.

What the Paddletails had to do first was to find

their new home. All the time they were wondering if after they found it they would like it as well as they did their old home.

Now if it had been Shaggy the Wolf or Reddy Fox who was going to the new home, it would not have taken either one of them long to go there, because it really was not a great distance. But the Paddletails were slow travelers, so it was not until the second night after they left the Flattails that they found it.

"I see it! I see it!" said Brownie, and, sure enough, there was the High Dam near enough so that the Paddletails could hear the Singing Water as it tumbled down over the sticks. In a little while the Paddletails scrambled up to the Wildwood Pond, and there they were at last. They had reached their new home.

It was rather a nice Wildwood Pond, but it was not so large as the one they had left, because the Flattails had not made such a High Dam.

"Oh, there is our new Brushy House!" said Silver; "let's swim over to it."

It had been quite a while since the Paddletails had been in water that was deep enough to play Dive and Spin in, and they had to stop for a play spell before they did anything else.

At last Paddletail swam over to the Brushy

House, dived down to the Secret Doorway, and went in. My, but you should have seen how surprised he was when he came up inside! Right there was a whole family of Beavers, and they had come to stay. Yes, sir; they had been on an excursion themselves, and had found the Brushy House.

Of course there was nothing for Paddletail to do but to leave, so he swam back and told Mrs. Paddletail about it. You see, the Flattails had gone away and left it, and it really belonged to the first ones that came.

"Now what shall we do?" asked Mrs. Paddletail.

"I wonder," said Paddletail, and he swam to the bank where he could eat some Spicy Bark while he thought it over. It surely was a problem.

Paddletail found a Quaking Aspen Tree that was already cut down, which just suited his taste, so he sat down to eat Spicy Bark and think. And do you know what he was thinking about?

Paddletail was thinking about his own Wildwood Pond on the Old Homestead, and about his Brushy House and High Dam. He was wondering if the High Dam needed repairing, and if the Flattails would keep it as nice as he did. For Paddletail was a good workman, and he was particular how things were done.

Then Paddletail thought about Danny Muskrat, and about the good times they had had together, and he wondered if Danny would like the Flattails as well. Those were some of the things that Paddletail was thinking about while he chewed the Spicy Bark; but he was thinking about something else also. When you hear what it was, you will be as much surprised as Mrs. Beaver was when he told her.

Said Paddletail to Mrs. Beaver: "Let's go back to our own Wildwood Pond in the Black Forest and build another Brushy House right by the first one. I know the Flattails will help us."

"That is a good idea, a very good idea," said Mrs. Paddletail.

"Oh, I am so glad we are going back to our own Wildwood Pond!" said Silver Paddletail.

"And so am I," said Brownie.

So the next night, after the Laughing Yellow Sun had winked good night in the Golden West, the Paddletails started back down Little River toward the Old Homestead. First there was Paddletail in the lead, and next was Mrs. Paddletail, and then Brownie Paddletail, and last came Silver.